Françoise Chaptain awoke to see a man looking down at her.

Early morning light at the barn door revealed a man with an ax resting across his shoulder, his face obscured in darkness. Françoise's mother and younger brother lay sleeping in the fresh hay on either side of her. She had reason to fear an unknown person, for she and her family were fleeing for their lives.

Her eyes widened in terror. The stranger could slay all three of the refugees on the spot. Civil war in France had increased in intensity the past few months. Who could know friend from foe? Sixteen-year-old Françoise gripped her mother's forearm and shook it gently.

BARBARA YOUREE has authored six children's books as well as numerous stories and articles. She was a contributing editor of *Potpourri, A Magazine of the Literary Arts,* and a docent at the Nelson-Atkins Museum of Art in Kansas City, Missouri. She now makes her home in Arkansas.

Books by Barbara Youree

HEARTSONG PRESENTS
HP416—Both Sides of the Easel
HP483—Forever Is Not Long Enough

Don't miss out on any of our super romances. Write to us at the following address for information on our newest releases and club information.

Heartsong Presents Readers' Service
PO Box 719
Uhrichsville, OH 44683

Or visit www.heartsongpresents.com

one

A farm west of Angoulême, France, 1572

"You are, indeed, a ragged bunch!"

Françoise Chaplain awoke to see a man looking down at her. Early morning light at the barn door revealed a man with an ax resting across his shoulder, his face obscured in darkness. Françoise's mother and younger brother lay sleeping in the fresh hay on either side of her. She had reason to fear an unknown person, for she and her family were fleeing for their lives.

Her eyes widened in terror. The stranger could slay all three of the refugees on the spot. Civil war in France had increased in intensity the past few months. Who could know friend from foe? Sixteen-year-old Françoise gripped her mother's forearm and shook it gently.

Her mother, Elise, awoke and sat up straight. "Pardon, monsieur. Please forgive us. My children and I sought refuge last night from the rain. We have taken nothing. Please, monsieur," she pleaded, "do not harm my children."

"That is not my intention," the man said with a thick Italian accent. He swung the ax from his shoulder and hung it beside other tools on the barn wall. Now weaponless, the man made the sign of the cross.

The boy of eleven sat up and rubbed his eyes. "Mamma, what—?"

"Shush, Etienne," the mother said. Françoise and her mother stood together, pulling straw from their tangled hair and straightening their skirts. "We will not bother you more but will be on our way," the older woman said.

"I am Pietro Marinelli," the man said. "Follow me."

5

Although the stone barn was attached to the living quarters, no door stood between the two. Françoise, having no other options, stepped out of the darkness with her bedraggled family and followed the farmer around to the front door. Her eyes squinted at the rim of sun that burst over the rounded hills.

"Wait here," Pietro Marinelli said. "I must forewarn my wife. She gets nervous at the sight of strangers. Not only do we not know our enemies, but we have heard rumors of the plague not far hence."

"We have not encountered the plague, monsieur," said the girl. With trembling fingers, she tied the loose strings of her cap under her chin and smoothed her torn skirt.

The rain had stopped during the night, and warm humidity rose in puffs of vapor from the valley. Françoise could hear the man and wife arguing in hushed Italian through the open window. In the distance, she could make out two figures approaching, apparently carrying long guns. "Oh, Mamma," Françoise said and threw her arms about her mother. "I do hope they hurry and let us in. I see two men over there, coming this way with weapons." Etienne stepped closer to his mother.

The master of the house reappeared in the doorway. "Come," he said. They followed him to an area behind the house secluded by vines and a pole fence. In the midst of the enclosure stood an empty rust-rimmed tub. "My wife is heating water for your baths and will provide dry clothes. This young one will have to roll up sleeves and the legs of breeches as we have nothing to fit him. Throw everything in a pile behind these bushes. I will burn them. We cannot be too careful with the possibility of contagion."

"There are two men. . . ," said Françoise, her voice quivering.

The man turned in the direction of the girl's darting eyes. "Oh, you need not worry. Those are my sons, coming from the fields with hoes resting on their shoulders. We try to get a couple of hours' work done before breakfast. They are clearing the south slope for a new vineyard. My sons will go first to the barn. Your privacy is secure here."

When he left, a stout woman appeared at the back door with two buckets of steaming water. Without a word, she poured the water into the tub. The three refugees stood silently as she brought more buckets. She set folded clothing on a stool next to the tub and placed a chunk of lye soap on top. Last of all, she brought two folded and pressed linen towels embroidered in a Venetian pattern. These were, Françoise guessed, prized possessions brought from Italy and reserved for honored guests.

"For you," the woman said, offering them to the mother without making eye contact. She pointed to the tub and the clothing. "For you," she repeated.

"Merci, madame," Françoise's mother said as she took the linens. "Thank you a million times over."

The woman smiled nervously. "I make you breakfast," she said and disappeared through the doorway.

For three weeks, they had walked in fear at night and hidden during daylight, carrying nothing but their sorrow with them. Françoise understood this woman's hesitancy around strangers.

She relished the warm bath and clean clothes. After dressing, she watched her brother energetically lather his brown curls. "I thought you enjoyed your disheveled appearance," she said with affection.

Although her clothes were torn from brambles and soiled from travel, she hesitated to relinquish them. But she knew they must obey the man's orders and leave them to be burned. Otherwise he couldn't be certain they were clean of the plague.

❧

To break the morning fast, Pietro Marinelli, his wife, Isabella, and their two grown sons, Stefano and Giulio, sat at the wooden plank table across from Françoise, her mother, and her brother. Strikingly taller than her mother, Françoise yet reflected her porcelain skin, dark lustrous hair, slender figure, and fine features. She felt sheltered here, though ill at ease in strange surroundings, customs, and unfamiliar dress. All remained silent until the father crossed himself and recited a short prayer.

Isabella Marinelli poured fresh milk from a pitcher into individual bowls for each person and passed around a loaf of bread from which each pulled an ample portion. A platter of sausages and a pot of grape jam sat in the center of the table.

Françoise knew the simple dress they had worn earlier—caps and capes and dark fabric—announced their origin. They couldn't hide the fact that they had fled from the Huguenot town of La Rochelle, recently attacked by the government. Before Pietro Marinelli could ask, Françoise's mother confessed they were fleeing refugees.

"If you have been walking since the raid on La Rochelle, you must be starved and certainly weary," the older man observed.

"Indeed, we are," said the mother. "We are so grateful for your hospitality. As we are not of your sect, you might have handed us over to the king's militia. Instead, you have kindly taken us in, fed, and clothed us, just as our Lord Jesus taught."

The refugees ate slowly. Françoise did not wish to appear greedy or impolite. Her mother had trained her and her brother well in gracious manners.

Their host dipped his wooden spoon into the pot of jam and spread it on his bread. "You see, we were once refugees also. When France and Spain were fighting to control Milan—that's where we are from—they destroyed my wool factory, broke the looms, terrified my weavers, then set fire to the place. That was in 1560—twelve years ago."

Françoise flinched at the mention of fire. She sipped her bowl of milk to hide her reaction. She felt awkward in Madame Isabella's cast-off dress with the sash twice wrapped around, though she savored the clean sun-dried smell of the fabric. Her discarded dark dress with white cape, indeed, had been the last thread of anything she owned. The odor of its burning wafted through the narrow window, increasing her fear of fire.

The man continued his story. "We tried to pursue the business in our home, but with Spain in power in Italy, commerce did not flourish. We struggled financially. Ever since your king Francis visited Italy, France has adored everything Italian, or so I had heard. Thus, I concluded the French would accept us and decided to move our family here for a fresh start."

Stefano had been as silent as his mother up to this point. "I was nine and my brother eight," he said. "We didn't know a word of French then." He looked directly across the table to Françoise. Their gazes met briefly. Then Françoise lowered her long eyelashes.

She rested in the calm offered at this table—one element so like the pleasant times in her memory of her own home. In spite of recent tragedies too heavy to bear, she could feel the young man's notice of her, being fully aware of the still damp ringlets of hair framing her face. The scooped neckline of the unfamiliar dress, though amply modest, brought her fingers to touch her throat lightly. For a moment, his attention pleased her. But the black cloud of sorrow swallowed up her small pleasure.

"I sent my little Italian boys to school in Angoulême just the same," the father boasted. "Within a year, Stefano was at the head of his class and Giulio not far behind. They were soon speaking French like natives. Now, at twenty-one, Stefano keeps all our farm ledgers and handles the family money. Giulio is most curious. He reads anything he can find and brings us news from the war when he goes into town. We left one place ravaged by war only to see other wars break out here. So far they have not conscripted my sons."

Etienne reached for another sausage, hesitated, and looked to his mother. She nodded and smiled, then turned toward Monsieur Pietro.

"Several French peasants befriended us," he continued. "One family took us into their home and shared what they had until we were able to purchase these twenty hectares that were being sold for back taxes. My vineyards have proven profitable, and the remoteness protects us."

"Remember the little black dog that family had? He loved my shoes and would hide them if I wasn't careful," said Giulio.

"I had a dog once," said Etienne.

No one said another word for several minutes. By their reverent silence, Françoise thought the Marinellis had some understanding of their suffering. Then the farmer said, "Indeed, you are not the first family we have found sleeping on the hay in our barn."

Isabella Marinelli cleared the table. When she finished, Stefano asked the guests, "How did you survive? It must be more than a hundred kilometers from La Rochelle to Angoulême. What did you eat, and where did you sleep?"

Still with downcast eyes, Françoise felt Stefano looking to her for answers to his questions. But she would keep the horrors locked forever within herself. Mamma would answer.

"Fortunately, in late summer, there are still vegetables in family gardens," said her mother, hesitating to reveal their circumstances. "We helped ourselves at night by moonlight. I reminded my children that the apostles of our Lord Jesus ate grains from the fields they passed when they were hungry. Much of the way, we walked along the Charente River, so we had water. Sometimes we took milk from a willing cow or goat. For safety, we slept during the heat of the day, concealed behind bushes, and traveled at night."

"We've heard the raid on La Rochelle was quite bloody— almost as bad as the recent massacre on St. Bartholomew's Day in Paris," said Giulio, the family's gatherer of news.

The composed demeanor of Françoise's mother collapsed. She burst into mournful sobs and rushed out the back door. Françoise saw her mother sit on the steps next to the tub and weep uncontrollably. She stared past her mother in silence.

"Giulio, my son, you do not need to say everything you

know," said his father in a gentle reprimand.

"Yes, Father."

"I can tell you about it," said Etienne, taking on the role of family spokesman. "The wars had been going on for as long as I can remember. We felt fairly safe in our houses, though. Mostly it was just fighting in the streets—throwing rocks, yelling insults. Right after the big massacre in Paris—a few days or so—whole regiments marched down the streets of our town. I peeked out the window and saw houses on fire. Then I saw about four or five soldiers running toward our house. I yelled for Father to get his sword."

Françoise noticed that Isabella Marinelli furrowed her brow in an apparent effort to follow the French.

"And did he attack them?" asked Giulio.

Etienne's face clouded. "No, they broke down the door and. . .shot Father. . .dead," he whispered.

The boy wiped his rolled-up sleeve across his face. "My sister's suitor was there in the front room and went to help Father, but they shot him, too. Françoise ran to him, but Mamma grabbed her arm and pulled her back. My two young sisters had been playing in the bedroom where my baby brother slept.

"We all tried to run in and save them, but soldiers stood in the doorway with swords drawn. The man with the gun pointed it at us and said, 'Run for your lives!' We did, and we could hear him laughing. I don't know why they didn't shoot us. When we looked back, our house was burning. They set it ablaze with the children still there. The windows in that room are high up. They couldn't have gotten out."

Tears ran down Etienne's contorted face. He rushed outside and threw his arms around their mother. Françoise remained still as stone.

"Françoise, I am so sorry," said Stefano softly.

"We all are," said Pietro Marinelli as he shook his head.

"I sorry." His wife reached out and placed her hand on the girl's shoulder.

The retelling brought fresh grief to Françoise. Pain had blocked much of the horrible scene, but she recalled a forgotten detail: Her suitor had acted aloof the days before his death. Irrationally, she had begun to distrust him—without finding a reason.

two

Her mother spent the day on the straw pallet offered her in the loft. Françoise knew her strength had held firm these past weeks for her children, and now that they were safe, her frail body demanded rest. She lay down next to her mother, rubbed her back and shoulders, knowing no words could comfort her. Indeed, her own grief equaled her mother's, but she possessed the strength of youth. When her mother fell asleep, Françoise descended the ladder to assist Isabella Marinelli with domestic chores. Few words were necessary between the women as Françoise understood the language of common tasks.

Etienne helped the men clear brush on the slope. At noon they all came in for the bean soup and bread the women had prepared. Françoise noticed the boy's ruddy cheeks glowed from his work.

"Etienne, you look a year older already," Françoise said as she tousled his hair.

"It's the big clothes, I guess," he said with a grin.

"He's a strong little worker," said Pietro Marinelli.

"And skillful with an ax," added Stefano. "Indeed, I would not wish to be his enemy."

Françoise smiled at his remark, though no one else appeared to catch his attempt at humor. "We had a small farm outside La Rochelle," she said. With the tragedy tucked deep inside, she now felt free to share more pleasant images. "We lived in town but raised wheat and vegetables. Etienne worked with my father out there and learned the use of the farm tools. Then they fished because we lived by the sea. Mamma and I took care of the goats we kept on the common ground. We made and sold the best goat cheese in the region."

"Mother makes wonderful goat cheese, too," said Stefano. Françoise noted his effort to draw commonalities between the two families.

"I make tomorrow," said Stefano's mother, her eyes lighting with real interest. "You help?" She smiled at Françoise.

"I will help."

"Today we make breeches to fit the boy."

Pietro Marinelli patted his wife's shoulder. "You are a good wife," he said.

❧

As the week passed, Françoise enjoyed working with her hostess, who seemed to accept her as an equal. She learned more from her and her husband about their wool business in Milan that brought in a comfortable income. But she spoke little about her own childhood in La Rochelle, where the Chaplains were respected leaders in the religious community. Her father had earned his bread as a humble fisherman, but the congregation esteemed him as a teacher of Holy Scripture. She remembered how he had taught her and her brothers to read, principally from the treasured Bible kept in their home.

It pleased her to see her brother engaged in work, helping the men with clearing the slope and setting out grape cuttings for a new vineyard.

Françoise was glad when her mother regained her strength. She joined her and Isabella Marinelli in processing the goats' milk in huge wooden tubs, patting the cheese into molds to store in the cellar for curing. Together, she and her mother sewed undergarments, and each altered the dress given her. Although her mother fashioned for herself a plain white cap in the Huguenot style, Françoise felt no need to do so. Her way of life before this was no more.

On the seventh day of their sojourn, the families lingered around the table after the evening meal. Suddenly, they heard the crunch of cart wheels on the pebbles near the cottage. Françoise glanced at her mother in alarm.

"It is only Giulio returning from market where he took our

produce this morning," said Stefano. "He, no doubt, brings us news. And I hope he shared none."

"Son, don't be accusing your brother," said his father.

"Yes, Father. I am just concerned because he tends to talk freely."

Françoise had noticed some friction between the two sons. The father overtly showed no favoritism, but his trust seemed most steady with Stefano. He kept a closer eye on his younger son.

❧

Stefano strode out the door to help his brother unbridle the mule and stow the sacks of flour and salt brought from town.

When the two had finished, Giulio burst into the room. "No plague in Angoulême after all!"

"Praise be to God," said his father.

Giulio pulled a chair up to the table as Stefano took his own place. "The eleven persons I reported sick last week have all recovered. Apparently it was another sort of fever. But I am sad to say that people are dying in Bordeaux—though the plague is not yet widespread there."

"That is not welcome news. Son, did you learn as to the time the boat leaves Bordeaux?"

"Yes, Father. Yes, I did. She is ready to sail down the Garonne day after the morrow morning. I sent word to our friend the captain to reserve places for the Chaplains."

"Good work," said his father.

Stefano chose not to react to Giulio's smirk as he gloated over his father's approval.

Françoise's mother tied a knot in the last stitch of her cap and laid it aside. "We shall be ready," she said. "Our only possessions will be the clothing we wear."

With Stefano's urging, his father had arranged a plan and presented it to the Chaplain family. They had agreed to seek refuge in the home of Stefano's uncle Matteo and his aunt Caterina. From fellow countrymen and other friends along the route, he and his family had recently received word of their relatives. Apparently, they were in need of women's help at their villa in Milan, Italy. As a merchant of fabrics, Uncle Matteo was often away, and his wife craved companionship since their daughter was married and gone.

"Stefano has agreed to accompany you to Bordeaux, where you will spend the night with Isabella's sister, Josephine. She and her husband live on this side of the town," explained the father.

Stefano leaned across the table toward Françoise and looked directly at her face. "Do not be fearful, Françoise. We have made the arrangements, as far as possible, for your journey."

Françoise met his gaze. "Thank you, Stefano. You are more than kind."

"And, Giulio, you have sent my message to Jacques?"

"Yes, Brother."

He turned back to Françoise and focused his gaze on her long, slender fingers, laced as in prayer, on the table. "Jacques is a friend of ours who runs a coach service from the Garonne River dock in Toulouse." Françoise withdrew her folded hands to her lap. "He will meet you there, take you by coach to the port in Narbonne, and arrange for your passage across the Mediterranean to Genoa."

Now addressing Françoise's mother, Stefano said, "Uncle Matteo has many connections. He even knows Cosimo, the Grand Duke of Tuscany. I trust him to find a way for your support. I wrote a letter to our uncle, and Giulio sent it by messenger a few days ago, after you agreed to the plan. If he has received it, he will meet you in Genoa. If not, I have written down instructions for hiring a coach in that city to take you on to Milan, along with directions written in Italian for the driver to follow to their villa."

"You have thought of every detail," said Françoise's mother. "We can never repay your kindness. But we shall certainly reimburse the financial expense when we are able."

"We are only repaying kindness shown me and my family by others. You owe me nothing," said his father. "You will find opportunities to do the same—I am sure of it."

"Will we sail in a big ship?" asked Etienne, who showed more excitement about the venture than his mother and sister.

"Not on the Garonne," said Giulio. "But when you cross the Mediterranean, that's a big one with sails and all. You may be seasick and have to heave over the sideboards." The boy laughed and mocked retching.

&

Over the week, Stefano had come to enjoy Etienne's presence and knew he would miss both his jokes and manly somberness. But Françoise he would miss with pain in his heart. And for their mother he held profound respect.

He listened closely as Françoise's mother looked to his family around the table. "This then is our last night in your abode. May I propose—rather, my children and I are in need of a praise service to God—in our manner—but we would be so privileged for you to be part of it, for we believe God sent us to you and, through you, provided our good fortune."

"Yes, certainly," said Stefano's father. "Show us your manner."

"I will begin with Scripture. The children will sing a psalm. Then we each will pray what is laid upon our hearts. It's all very simple."

Stefano and his family nodded in agreement.

As dusk had settled, his mother lit the eight candles in the candelabra on the table.

Françoise's mother stood and recited from memory the first epistle of Paul to the Corinthians, chapter 13: "Though I speak with the tongues of men and of angels, and have not charity, I am become as sounding brass, or a tinkling cymbal. . . ." She continued without pause to the last verse. "And now abideth faith, hope, charity, these three; but the greatest of these is charity."

When her mother finished, Françoise took Etienne's hand, and they stood together. She began singing Psalm 61. Her brother joined in. "Hear my cry, O God; attend unto my prayer. From the end of the earth will I cry unto thee, when my heart is overwhelmed: lead me to the rock that is higher than I. . . ."

Stefano sat transfixed. Never had he heard a more angelic voice. Without question, he already held feelings for the French girl who had graced their home. But as he listened to the duo—for, in fact, Etienne's voice was gifted, as well—he knew this feeling was nothing less than love.

&

Stefano and the others arose well before dawn. He thought only of Françoise and her family as he and his brother tended to the milking and feeding of livestock. When he returned to the house, his mother was helping Françoise and her mother pack food for the long day's journey. They lined each of two deep baskets with an extra petticoat and other such essentials. On top of the clothing, they arranged loaves of bread, fruit, cheese, and strips of dried beef.

Stefano took Madame Elise's suggestion that Etienne, now the surviving male of the family, be entrusted with carrying the necessary funds. Like him, the boy showed a gift for mathematics and, thus, he felt, could be responsible for the accounting.

When Stefano had finished his chores, he went to a hidden cache in the barn and filled a leather pouch full of gold coins. He brought it in and called the boy. "Etienne, come see the actual coins of which I spoke last night." He emptied out the gold pieces on the table. Etienne rushed to touch the Italian scudi.

"You know the French francs and their value. You will use these for your family's expense up to Narbonne and for the ship's fare to cross the Mediterranean." Stefano then gave him a lesson in recording and subtracting expenditures. His mother and sister stood by and listened as well. "Write everything on this little tablet with the quills. Here is a small vial of ink. And now for the gold scudi," said Stefano as he separated them from the francs.

He explained to the boy the value of the pieces and how

much to expect to pay for a coach, a night's lodging, and food items. "Never show all your money," he warned. "Have ready the coins in your hand that you expect to pay. That way it will be easier to bargain."

Etienne gathered the money and returned it to the leather pouch, then stuffed in the paper, quills, and ink. As he tied the bundle to his belt, Stefano's father brought a floppy velvet cap, dusted it off, and placed it on Etienne's head.

"How like a dapper businessman you look!" exclaimed the boy's mother.

"A coif for the girl, too," said Isabella Marinelli, suddenly leaving the room and returning with a little lace cap. "For you," she said to Françoise, "from Milan."

"Merci, madame," said Françoise. "You have been so kind to us. May God richly bless you and your family for your goodness."

With her mother's help, she attached the cap over the circle of braids that crowned her head. Dark ringlets hung at the sides of her face. The pale blue dress fit snugly at the pointed waist and flared to full length. She stood in the center of the room, her hands clutching a small handkerchief. The full, puffed sleeves hid healing scratches—that Stefano had noticed before—from rough travels across the countryside.

For a frozen moment in time, Stefano stared at this beautiful creature who had bloomed in the single week under the Marinelli roof. Although he would accompany the family to Bordeaux, this image of her standing in his home imprinted itself in Stefano's mind. He resolved not to allow her to slip away from him forever.

three

Françoise had grown fond of their hostess and parted in sadness with embraces and kisses to both cheeks in the French custom. She, her mother, and Etienne shared warm handshakes with Giulio and his father. Conflicting emotions overcame Françoise as she climbed into the mule-drawn cart beside her mother—fear of the unknown, gratitude for recent kindness, haunting memories of the murders of loved ones, dread of dangers on the journey. *At least Stefano will be with us awhile longer*, she thought to console herself.

Once the two women were settled in the cramped cart, baskets on their laps, Stefano mounted the one horse owned by the family. Etienne jumped on behind him. A dagger hung conspicuously at Stefano's side. Two jugs of water tied together straddled the back of the horse. The boy was charged with a large bag of cheeses to be sold in Bordeaux.

Slowly, the little group wended its way to the crest of a hill. As streaks of red and gold announced dawn in the eastern sky, Françoise turned to look back at the cottage in the distance. She could just make out the figures of the older Marinellis standing at the doorway.

Where are we going, and what will become of us? My life—for however long it may last—lies before me, but all I see is darkness. Then words from her favorite psalm came to mind: *"My heart is overwhelmed: lead me to the rock that is higher than I."* It brought no brightness to the future, but it did calm her anxious spirit.

⁓

The day proved long and tedious with little beyond unfamiliar scenery to amuse them. A few times Stefano asked Françoise to sing psalms, but with the mule and cart trailing him, she had to strain to be heard. She was glad they encountered no bandits or government militia—only a few other weary travelers like them. The wooden wheels bumped along over the deep ruts and rocks, making riding uncomfortable. They stopped to eat only twice and to stretch and give the animals a break thrice more. Françoise's neck and leg muscles ached with stiffness. Dust filled her nostrils and left a film of grime over everything, but fortunately, the overcast sky kept out much of the heat of the day.

When it grew dark, Stefano lit a lantern that swung from a pole at the front of the cart, casting eerie light among the shadows. Now the mule and cart led the way with the only light. Somehow Françoise felt safer with Stefano behind, protecting them from any rear attack. They arrived at their destination well into the night.

They had had no way to notify their hosts, Aunt Josephine and her husband, in time; thus, when Stefano clanged the bell at the gate, a response was slow in coming. Finally, a sleepy-eyed and disgruntled-looking stable boy arrived.

"What ye be doing here?" He yawned. "The master's gone to Royan an' won't be back 'til the morrow eve. Come back then." He turned to leave.

"I am Stefano Marinelli, the nephew of the master's wife, Madame Josephine."

This jarred the boy into alertness. He took a large key from his belt and unlocked the gate. "In that case, m'sieur, I'll wake m'dame and announce your visit." With that, he ran up the long path and pounded the knocker on the front door. In a few minutes, he returned to take the horse, mule, and cart to the stables.

"G'on up, m'sieur. The maid—she's at the door and will let you in."

The maid stood in the doorway of the manor with lighted candle in hand. "You are welcome," she said. "Please come in and sit down. I will serve refreshments. Madame will be with you shortly." She lit several candles and disappeared.

"It is late," said Françoise's mother, wiping dust from her

brow with a handkerchief as they all stepped inside. "I hope we have not terribly inconvenienced her."

Etienne looked around wide-eyed at the large paintings on the walls, the sconces with lit candles, and the brocaded furniture. "This is a very grand house," he said. "They must be well off."

"Yes, my aunt's husband is a winegrower. He owns several vineyards outside the city. Aunt Josephine came with us from Milan. She was barely fifteen then and married shortly afterward."

The little group stood in the middle of the room rather than sit on the fine furniture with their dusty garments. Françoise, fatigued from travel, wanted only to sleep.

Suddenly Madame Josephine bustled into the room in dressing gown and slippers. "Welcome to our home, dear Stefano!" She embraced him and kissed his cheeks. "And who are these dear people? This lovely young lady? She must be your betrothed. Why didn't you let us know? Isabella must adore her. And what is your name, mademoiselle?"

She rushed toward Françoise with the apparent intent of embrace. Françoise instinctively recoiled—and felt her cheeks burn at the thought of betrothal.

"No, no, dear aunt, these are friends. Madame Elise Chaplain is a recent widow. This is her daughter, Françoise, and her son, Etienne. I am escorting them to the port tomorrow."

"He didn't die of the plague, I hope." Now Stefano's aunt pulled back as Françoise had. "Or are they escaped Huguenots? Those people are overrunning our country. They'll have their Henri on the throne—mark my words. They are a bunch of power grabbers trying to take over France."

"Don't worry, Aunt Josephine. No cases of plague have shown up in Angoulême. Besides, since our farm is some distance from the town, our isolation protects us."

Françoise smiled at the clever way Stefano avoided answering her rude questions directly. How very unlike his mother this woman was! She resembled her sister only in features and plumpness. But she certainly had gained a better grasp of the French language and could use it liberally.

"Humph. Marie, bring cloths to put on the chairs so these guests may properly sit down."

"Oh, we don't need to—" began Françoise's mother, her voice revealing discomfort.

Marie brought the cloths as well as a board of cheese and bread and a refreshing drink. They sat briefly on the protected furniture and engaged in polite, empty conversation. Stefano offered the gifts of jam and cheese his mother had sent. As soon as Marie had prepared washbasins and other necessities in the bedrooms, they all retired.

Because the travelers' baskets appeared too small to hold much clothing, Marie laid out white gowns for the two ladies and a nightshirt for the boy. After sponging off the journey's grime and shaking their clothes out the window, Françoise's mother sank into the featherbed and fell fast asleep. Likewise, Etienne's adjoining alcove soon became quiet.

But, in spite of exhaustion, Françoise lay wide-awake, drowning in the overstuffed and unfamiliar bed. Flashbacks of their house in flames haunted her. She squeezed her eyes tightly shut, but sleep would not come. She imagined the horrible last minutes of her little sisters' and brother's lives. She saw them frantically trying to escape, pounding on the door, trying to reach the high window; the oldest girl, barely four, holding the screaming baby; their finally dying alone in agonizing pain. Sometimes she would imagine the room simply filled with smoke, cutting off their breath, followed by a few coughs, and their drifting off to sleep. But she knew pain was more likely. She tossed about, finding no escape.

Finally, afraid of waking her mother in the next bed, she got up. Moonlight shone through the open window. Her reflection in the looking glass startled her—the white gown floating like a ghost. Marie had left a peignoir hanging by the mirror. She started to put it on, then thought she might appear immodest if she encountered Stefano's aunt.

Instead, she slipped her dusted-off dress over the gown and descended the stairway barefoot. Much to her surprise, a light still burned in the sitting room. She was well into the room before realizing she was not alone. Stefano sat reading by a whale-oil lamp.

"Françoise? Are you all right?" he whispered without moving.

"Yes. I suppose so," she whispered back. "I could not sleep. I didn't know you were here. I don't mean to disturb you. I'll leave you to your reading. . . ."

"No, please stay." He closed the book and waved his hand toward the chair on the other side of the lamp table. "My aunt was less than gracious tonight. I am sorry for her words."

She sat on the cushioned chair and crossed her bare ankles. Of course, it was indiscrete to be here alone with a young man. In the entire week they stayed at his house, not once had the two of them been alone. But tonight she didn't care; no one would know, and certainly Stefano was a gentleman. She wanted to pour out the agony of her memories, but her heart remained closed. Instead she said, "You were quick witted enough to protect us. I suppose your aunt would not have let us stay if she had known we were Huguenots."

"Possibly not. But her remark was meant for me. She is angry at my father for taking in refugees from the war who come our way—from both sides."

"Why is he—your whole family—so good? Surely you know how dangerous it is. The government could arrest you for harboring us, for bringing us here." For the first time, she realized the Marinellis were just as vulnerable to retaliation by the government's faction as her family.

"My father is a man of great faith. He believes God has directed him to befriend any refugee brought to him. He arranges for them to go to Geneva or Amsterdam. Others also help out along the way. But this is the first time he has sent a family to his brother in Milan. I think he was especially touched by your plight. He believes that whether we live or die, we are the Lord's." He paused, then turned to another subject. "Françoise, are you worried about the future?"

"Yes, and the past."

"Would you like to talk about what's troubling you?" The lamplight reflected in his eyes as he looked directly into hers. Throughout the long, tiring trip, she had hardly thought of him. She had passed the time with concerns about her mother's discomfort—or her own—and fought off the tormenting memories. Now she focused her attention on this young man whose family had done so much for them. The face looking at her, indeed, was a handsome one, clean shaven with fine Italian features. His ill-managed dark hair grew barely past the ruff of his collar. One wayward lock fell across his forehead. And his hands, rough from manual labor, still held the book—*Poems of the Italian Renaissance*.

"Do you like poetry?" she said after several minutes, ignoring the question put to her.

"Yes, it helps me see life more clearly. This is one of my aunt's books. I love to come here and read from their library. We have so few books at home."

"We had only the Holy Scriptures. My father taught Etienne and me to read from it," she confided and checked to make sure the gown didn't show at the top of her dress.

"Tell me about your father."

"He was a good man but very strict when it came to lessons. He also taught us arithmetic, some history, and geography. He had a map of Europe and a book called *The New World* that he borrowed from a friend. He taught me to play the harpsichord—"

"Your family had a harpsichord?" Stefano's eyes widened.

"Well, yes, we should not have had one. Huguenots generally do not use musical instruments. When the iconoclasts took over the church, destroying the statues, icons, and instruments of music, my father and older brother slipped the harpsichord out a back door onto a waiting goat cart." She could see Stefano's amusement and chuckled with him. "They threw a rug over it and brought it home! Thus it was saved from destruction."

"Very clever, I say. But where is your older brother? I didn't know. . ."

Françoise sank back in her chair and sighed heavily from an unspoken pain. Several minutes passed. As if alone and unaware of Stefano's presence, she spoke aloud one of her fond memories.

"I would play for hours on Sunday afternoons, as we did little work on the Lord's Day. My father had just started teaching me to play the lute so I could accompany. . ." Her voice trailed off.

"You loved your father very much?"

"I mustn't talk more of him." Her voice choked. She closed her eyes, but the tears trickled down from the corners. Now back in the present, she turned toward Stefano and whispered, "I must go—back upstairs."

They both stood, facing each other. "Someday I will come to Milan, Françoise," he said and dared to put his hand beneath her chin and tilt her face up toward him. "I will never forget you and will pray always for your safety and happiness."

"I can promise you nothing," she said and broke into uncontrolled sobs.

Stefano, who had never held a woman before, wrapped his arms about her and pulled her close. After several moments of weeping, she relaxed and returned his embrace.

"There, there. I wish I could take away all your hurt and pain," he said. He released her and walked beside her to the foot of the stairs.

She turned and touched his arm. With a faint smile, she whispered, "Good night."

"Good night," he said. "Sleep well."

This time, as Françoise sank into the featherbed, she gave in to its fluffy embrace. Grieving emotions as well as the tingling of tenderness quite exhausted her, and she fell asleep in the imagined arms of Stefano.

four

Hours later, Françoise awoke refreshed and, along with her mother and brother, broke her fast with Stefano and his aunt Josephine in the enclosed courtyard garden. Stefano told his aunt that, after settling the family on the boat, he would return to her manor and await the arrival of his uncle. He would stay a couple of days, give assistance where needed, purchase supplies to take back in the mule cart, and read in the evenings.

This morning Madame Josephine chattered away while they ate, sharing gossip about people Françoise neither knew nor cared about. She felt shy sitting across from Stefano. She wondered if he remembered—in the same depth of detail as she—the embrace of the night before. Most of all, it had given her comfort—which she had accepted as his pure intent—but she ached for that again.

Like her mother, she responded to Madame Josephine's monologue with smiles and feigned interest: "I see." "Oh, is that so?" *How much longer can this woman prattle on?*

Finally, when his aunt paused for breath, Stefano turned to Françoise's mother. "I will pray always for your safety and happiness." Françoise recognized the exact words from the night before. Was this a trite phrase he said to everyone on departure, or was he repeating it now to her mother to emphasize his sincerity? "And that of your children," he added, looking first at Françoise, then at Etienne.

"Thank you," said her mother. "And we will pray equally for you."

At that moment, Stefano's aunt audibly gasped when the stable boy appeared in the doorway, having come through the house and into the private courtyard. Before she could utter a reproof, he blurted out his message. "M'dame, I've jus ben warned, an' I mus' warn you. Officers are knocking on all the doors. They will be here right soon."

"What officers? What has come over you, my boy?" snarled Madame Josephine.

"They say the dreadful sickness is nearby. They say no strangers can come or go. So if it's go your guests mean to do, they must do so quick."

They all stood. Stefano kissed his aunt on both cheeks. "We will leave immediately. Giulio has already arranged passage on the boat."

"Your horse and mule are ready at the gate, m'sieur."

Madame Josephine tossed the remaining breakfast bread and fruit into the ladies' baskets and ushered them out the front door.

Françoise's mother hastily thanked the woman for her hospitality and whispered to her son, "Do you have the coins, Etienne?"

"Yes, Mamma." He mounted the horse behind Stefano. His mother handed him the refilled water jugs and bag of cheeses. The ladies took their places in the cart, and they were off to the port of Bordeaux.

❧

As the group approached the port, Françoise noticed it was busy with what appeared to be prosperous commerce. But when they drew their animals to a halt, she realized that rather than merchants, all sorts of people had come in a frantic effort to escape the city. The faces of those leaving the dock all held the same expression of disappointment and desperation.

"You needn't go farther, monsieur," a man said to Stefano. "This boat's booked. Won't be another for two days unless you can take a ship to Spain." He wandered off, not waiting for a reply.

"Wait here," Stefano said in a calm voice. "Our family knows the captain, and Giulio made arrangements." With that, he handed Françoise the reins of his horse and headed toward the boat, Etienne in tow.

"Mamma, what if. . . ?" Françoise said, then noticed her mother's hands folded in prayer. She still sat in the cart. Françoise stood holding the reins of the horse and looked about her. The crowd consisted of people of all ages milling about. She wondered about the story of each: an aged woman with only a small parcel of possessions, a family with several bundles and as many children, a nobleman swaggering about with dress sword at his side. A toddler laughed with delight as he found shining pebbles and stuffed them inside his shirt.

Then she gasped at a truly gruesome sight. A man, with his back to her, lay on the ground groaning. At first she thought him to be a poor vagrant, but his clothing belied that assumption. He suddenly rolled to his back and flung his arms out wide. Sweat drenched his hair and collar. On his neck, a purple knot, large as a man's fist and filled with pus, threatened to burst. Rosy circles, like petals, splotched his face and hands. "Water. Water, please," he moaned. The crowd moved away from him, isolating his misery. An odor of rotting apples hung in the air.

Françoise thought of Stefano's words of last night about how his father felt compelled to help all refugees God sent to him. Was this poor soul sent to her for help?

Her mother sat watching him as well. "Daughter, those red spots are plague tokens. We could take him some of our water."

"Yes, Mamma." She reached to unfasten the water jugs.

At that moment, a woman about thirty, like the man, hurried to his side. She knelt beside him with a small pitcher and poured a few sips of water on his parched lips. A boy of about twelve came running with a folded blanket, lifted the man's head, and tucked it underneath. The nasty lump split open and spewed forth its ugly contents. Françoise almost retched at the sight. Both mother and daughter turned away. "There is nothing we can do," said her mother with a finality that relieved Françoise of her Christian duty.

They could hear the grieving sobs of the wife and son behind them as Stefano and Etienne walked up.

"You have passage," Stefano announced.

"But we had to pay double," said Etienne, patting the pouch of money tied to his belt.

"Everyone wants to get out of town because of the plague," said Stefano. "The water level of the Garonne is low, so only small barges such as the one you will take can navigate. Ships are going out to sea, but few people are prepared to pay that expense." Stefano explained the obvious. "You will have to go up to the boat by yourselves. I cannot leave my cart and animals. Many people become thieves when times are desperate. The captain will recognize Etienne. There will be no problem."

As Etienne pulled his bag of cheese from the horse's back, a man approached. "Is that cheese you have there?"

"Yes, I intend to sell it," said Etienne.

"Well, I'll buy the whole lot. I'm a vendor here and have already sold my foodstuff. This crowd will buy most anything. They have their money on them."

Françoise watched her brother haggle the price. The sale would in some small measure make up for having to pay double for their passage. She believed Etienne held his own like a regular merchant.

The man carried away his purchase, and Etienne counted his francs. "I suppose I could have made more selling them one at a time along the trip. But I thought about how awful cheese can smell in close quarters."

"You did very well," said Stefano.

Françoise glanced over at the man who apparently had just died. Two men were hoisting him onto a waiting cart. At least two other dead bodies had already been gathered into it. The woman unfolded the blanket laid under his head and gently spread it over her husband.

"What a tragedy," said Françoise. "The plague is truly an evil disease." This first encounter with the contagion left her with shock and fear—shock at its awfulness, fear that her mother, her brother, or she might be stricken with it.

"I must bid you farewell for a time," she heard Stefano say. He was shaking her mother's hand.

She turned, and her gaze met his. He took her hand in both of his—more of a caress than a shake. "May God's richest blessings rest upon you and keep you from all harm until we meet again."

"Until we meet again," said Françoise softly. "Good-bye."

"Good-bye," he said.

He gave Etienne a hug about the shoulders. "Manage well the money entrusted to you, my lad."

The three trudged toward the dock, lugging their baskets and water jugs. Halfway there, Françoise paused to look back. A young couple with a baby were climbing into Stefano's mule cart. He looked up and waved. *Stefano is such a good man, just like his father. Instead of a few pleasant days with his relatives, he will take this family in need of transport wherever they must go.*

❧

The flatboat trip on the muddy Garonne proved an arduous journey of over two weeks. The dozen passengers lacked both comfort and privacy. Françoise and the others sat among the merchandise in the cabin during the day and slept at night on the planks. The one square sail rarely caught enough wind to propel her along. Since the boat of necessity had to be poled upstream, they anchored her at night with ropes tied to trees. Twice the passengers were let off in villages to buy food. Etienne traded the two empty baskets for a small satchel.

One late afternoon, they docked at Toulouse. Leaving their mother to rest under a nearby shade tree, Françoise and Etienne asked around the port for Jacques, who owned a coach transport service. The third person they approached pointed out a young, talkative fellow standing next to his coach.

"Ah, so you are the Chaplains sent me by Signore Pietro Marinelli. Can you tell me how the family fares?" Jacques asked.

"Indeed, we left them in good health," said Françoise. Their mother joined them then.

"We hear the plague is raging in Bordeaux. Did you, by chance, encounter any of those afflicted?" He frowned and looked down as if embarrassed to ask.

Françoise knew he wanted to find out if they carried the seeds of the fever.

"No, we have not been in contact with the contagion," her mother said with confidence. After all, they had not been so close to the dying man.

"That is good. Many of the innkeepers refuse to take in anyone coming from Bordeaux," he said. "I know an innkeeper, however, who will take you on my recommendation."

With that, the family climbed into his carriage and soon arrived at the destination. Jacques introduced them to the innkeeper. "Ah, how pleasant to take in two decent women and a boy—rather than the carousers who often come here." Etienne made no argument over the price. Françoise agreed it seemed reasonable according to what Stefano had written on the little tablet.

"On the morrow I will come by for you at ten of the clock when I return from a short transport," said Jacques as he left.

Françoise sighed with relief that at last they could enjoy a good meal, bathe, and sleep on beds. In their room, the family quoted Scripture, softly sang psalms, and praised God for bringing them safely this far.

Tired but refreshed, Françoise lay in the dark and thought of her future. The coach trip overland would take three days. A Spanish galleon—a true ship with grand sails—would carry them across the Mediterranean to Genoa, Italy. There they might or might not meet up with Matteo Marinelli, Signore Pietro's brother. She must get used to the Italian way of speaking. Most likely they would be on their own to find their way to Milan and the Marinelli villa.

Françoise envisioned her new life with both fear and anticipation. Signore Matteo and his wife, Caterina, were, no doubt, generous and gracious like Signore Pietro and his wife. Stefano had described his aunt as lonely and craving companionship. They would help this woman in every way possible. Somehow they would find an industry to earn their way. Certainly she didn't wish to remain dependent for long.

Perhaps her mother would remarry. What a strange thought! Financially that would be good, but she could not bring herself to imagine her mother with anyone else. She thought of her own suitor, Guillaume, shot by the same soldier who murdered her father. *I remember I loved him, but I don't feel that love now. I feel certain he was one of the iconoclasts and betrayed us. There is no room for the emotion of love in my heart. It has been drained by the evils that have taken away all that was dear to me. I dare not love again.* But she fell asleep with the comfort of knowing that Stefano would be praying for her safety and happiness.

five

Stefano waited at the port of Bordeaux until he saw the single mast of the flatboat move away from the dock. In his heart, he committed the Chaplain family to the mercies of God. And he prayed especially for Françoise, that she would find some pleasure in her life so fraught with tragedy. From their brief time together at his aunt's house that night, he guessed it would be difficult to win her love. Yes, she responded to his touch, but she seemed so completely consumed by her burdens. He resolved to win her love, however long that might take.

A young couple sat patiently in his mule cart, bouncing and caressing their baby girl. He learned their names were Claire and Gaston. They had come to Bordeaux only recently to work in the grape harvest. Now they were desperate to return to his parents' farm that lay not far from the road he would travel. They were simple folk: he—short and stocky; she—scarcely older than a child herself, thin, and plain faced.

❧

Stefano found the trip more pleasant than traveling alone. With the baby, more stops were necessary for tending and nursing. At noon they spread a cloth on the grass by the road. The couple shared their parcel of bread and fruit with Stefano, as he had thought it best not to buy supplies in disease-stricken Bordeaux.

As the shadows grew long, Gaston invited Stefano to stay the night when they arrived at his parents' farmhouse. Claire seemed to protest the idea by nudging her husband in the ribs, but he ignored her objection. Indeed, with their late start and this added side trip to take them home, Stefano was glad to accept. A night's rest would be good.

During their stops, Gaston eagerly conversed on many topics: the war, the plague, the bountiful grape harvest, the fair wages they had received. Stefano carefully avoided expressing any opinions on the war to avert the slightest suspicion of his family's aid to refugees. His father had often warned his sons to guard their tongues in this regard.

As the party approached the farmhouse, Stefano could make out the silhouette of a man standing in the yard, his hands on his hips. With the sun setting in the hazy sky behind the figure, Stefano could not determine the expression on his face. But his words soon made clear his anger. "Gaston, what are you doing back here? We have little enough to eat as it is! If you hadn't been sucked in by this wench, you could have been some use to me. Now there are two more mouths to feed. For what are you here? You couldn't get hired out in Bordeaux? You worthless simpleton! And who's this useless filcher?"

Stefano acknowledged that would be himself. He stretched out his hand, but the man ignored the gesture.

Claire flinched at the string of oaths that followed this outburst. The man turned and stomped back into his hut. With its disintegrating thatch roof and only two rooms—plus the attitude of his host—Stefano could plainly see his lodge would be under the trees this night.

He helped Claire, with babe in arms, from the cart. "I hope it's not been too cramped a ride," Stefano said cheerfully, his temper unchanged by the unwelcome reception.

"No, no. Not at all. Thank you," she said and hurried to the arms of her mother-in-law, who had just emerged from the doorway. With tears in her eyes, the older woman tenderly took her grandchild.

Gaston grabbed the family bundle, his eyes anxiously glancing toward the doorway. "We are so grateful to you. Here—take this." He offered Stefano a small bag of coins. "I'd thought my father would be more forgiving. I'm sorry for his words."

Stefano refused the payment. "It wasn't much out of my way. Just help the next person that asks of you. Besides, I enjoyed your company, my good man."

"Then I thank you with all my heart. Excuse me, monsieur. I must go make peace with my father."

Stefano attached a rope to the mule's bridle to lead him alongside his horse. He was mounting when Gaston's mother came up to him, still holding the baby.

"You must stay and sup with us. I have just made a hearty soup. Gaston will tend to your animals. My husband often is thrown into a rage. He's angry that Gaston married so suddenly. But he is my only child that lived past infancy. And now we have this healthy little one. Isn't she a sweet thing?" The woman lapsed into baby talk, chucking her finger under the child's chin.

Stefano could smell the soup cooking in a pot hung over an open fire in the yard. He dismounted for, indeed, he was hungry. "I will stay if you like," he said.

"Please do. I'm sure Gaston will explain good reasons for their coming back to us. I promise you my husband will be civil once his stomach is full."

Claire had stood silently beside her mother-in-law. Now she placed her hand on the woman's arm. "The plague has come to Bordeaux. That is the reason for our return. I couldn't bear to lose our little one, and it's the children who suffer most."

❧

Stefano and the family sat on logs in front of the hut. The man, sullen at first, became talkative after several spoonfuls of soup. He expressed anger over many things, but at least it was no longer directed toward those present.

After sunset, a chill hung in the air. Stefano, following the lead of the others, moved closer to the fire for warmth and light.

"You make a fine vegetable soup, madame," said Stefano in all sincerity.

"Thank you, monsieur. There is a straw mattress in the front room where you may rest tonight."

Stefano accepted the offer as there seemed to be no objection from her husband, who continued to lash out against the evils of the world.

"I tell you," he said, "these Huguenots are taking over our country. They are a bunch of heretics who dishonor religion."

Stefano thought of Françoise's angelic voice singing psalms.

"They think they are better than the rest of us. Even their peasant children can read and do figures."

Monsieur Chaplain taught his children to read from the Bible. And little Etienne is so adroit with numbers. That is good.

"They desecrate our churches and tear up our musical instruments."

Stefano smiled, remembering the story Françoise told of her father and brother saving the harpsichord from destruction. But he said nothing.

"And let me tell you this, young man. There is a rough bunch of our own aiding these refugees as they escape retribution. Right here in the countryside around Angoulême there is a network of such folks."

"What have you heard?" Stefano's voice spoke mild curiosity that masked the alarm he felt.

"The news traveled through the marketplace in Angoulême a few days ago. An Italian fellow was overheard boasting to a mate that his family didn't care who they helped in the war—that meaning they helped Huguenots. The government forces arrested a Dutchman not too long ago who's part of this bunch of traitors. They'll make him talk, they will. He'll give up the information to save his skin."

"Is that so?" said Stefano. Suddenly he felt very tired with the burden of the knowledge he must carry to his father. The "Italian fellow" could well be Giulio.

&

Sleep came in only brief snatches, so bothered was Stefano by the news that put his family in jeopardy—and by the fleas and rats about his straw mat. Several times he sat up and prayed for God's direction in the new crisis he faced. And, as always, for the safety and happiness of Françoise as well as her mother and brother. Over and over, he relived the warm embrace they had shared. He felt her relax in his arms, then respond to him with her arms wrapped around his body. Surely they would be like this again someday—and more. Boldly, he prayed God would grant him this reunion.

He arose at first cockcrow, stuffed a chunk of bread—offered by Gaston—in his shirt, said his adieus, and headed toward the road.

He arrived home around midday. After feeding and giving water to the horse and mule, he scanned the horizon for his father and brother. He wished to speak to them before greeting his mother. As expected, he found them coming across the fields for the noon rest. He ran to meet them.

"Stefano, my son, so you got our little family off to Milan?" said his father as he wiped sweat from his brow.

"Yes, Father, but our lives may well be in peril!"

"Why? Is a bandit chasing you?" said Giulio. He laughed and looked around in mock search for the peril.

Stefano felt his face flush with outrage. Until this moment, he had tried hard not to direct the blame toward his brother, but now this taunting attitude enraged him.

"You, Giulio, you are the peril!" His teeth clenched, and he spit out the words. "They say an Italian man in Angoulême has been talking about harboring refugees. That man would be you, would it not?"

"I—I—" Giulio turned sober at the accusation.

"Giulio, is this true?" their father said in a tense voice. "I always warn you to guard your tongue. Even the walls have ears in time of war."

"I don't think I've revealed anything. I don't remember saying anything about it." He sounded both defensive and uncertain.

"Well, they know there is a network around Angoulême. They've already arrested a Dutchman. That would be our friend Hans."

Their father, now calm and calculating, said, "We must leave immediately. All of us are vulnerable, my sons. Let's have no more talk of blame. We must think and plan quickly. But first we must pray for direction."

The three men dropped to their knees among the dried potato vines. The father lifted his voice to heaven. "Almighty God, look with favor on us, Your servants. We have only done what we feel You have asked us to do—taken in the stranger, fed the hungry, cared for the wounded. Our lives and fortunes are in Your hands. Direct us in what we must do. Whatever befalls us, we will always trust in You. In the name of the Father and of the Son and of the Holy Spirit."

"Amen," said the three. They rose and crossed themselves.

"What will become of our farm, our goats, and cattle?" asked Giulio.

"We need to find someone we can trust," their father said.

"I know a young couple who lives with the husband's parents, not far from here. Gaston is his name, a good man. They need their own lodging. I believe he is capable—he could care for the vineyards and livestock—perhaps for a share of the profits," said Stefano.

"That is good. Contact him today," said his father. "We must get Isabella to her sister in Bordeaux. Josephine will accept her."

"She will not harbor us, Father," said Stefano.

"I know, my son. We are fugitives!"

six

Françoise found the crossing of the Mediterranean Sea an exciting adventure, but it seemed even more so for Etienne. When a rainstorm came up one evening, the captain called on all able-bodied young men to help man the sails. Etienne quickly volunteered. He even told Françoise he desired to become a sailor when he grew older.

Only their mother suffered from seasickness. But that passed after a few bouts in the beginning. They made friends with several congenial passengers. One Italian family, who lived in Genoa, had connections in France and crossed the sea once or twice a year. Thus, their French was almost as good as their Italian. They spent hours with Françoise and her mother, teaching them essential Italian phrases and customs. Françoise had picked up a few expressions over the week with the Marinelli family, but she had worried about communication in their new surroundings. She remembered how Stefano's mother struggled with French even after so many years in the country. Etienne found his own companions among the children on board and seemed to learn the new language quickly and effortlessly. Françoise disembarked with high hopes for her new life.

She and her family stood at the port in Genoa, hoping someone named Matteo Marinelli would approach them. But no such person appeared. This did not surprise Françoise. Even if he and his wife had received the message from his brother, how could he know what day they would arrive?

Etienne's Italian proved good enough to hire a coach in the direction of Milan. But Françoise noticed it was more difficult for him to bargain a good price. His foreign accent put him at a disadvantage. And she could be of little help. He encountered the same problem at the inn on the way and in hiring a second coach to take them the rest of the way into the city. Françoise reminded him to give the driver the written directions to the villa that Stefano had supplied for him. Fortunately, that was easily understood.

Françoise gawked in all directions at their first views of the city of Milan with its wide streets and ancient, as well as new, buildings. They passed a marketplace overflowing with sumptuous fruits and vegetables, grains, and slaughtered animals—and vendors hawking these wares. Crowds of people bustled about.

"It seems a prosperous city," said Françoise, enthralled with the prospect of living here.

"Indeed, it is," said the driver. "Did you notice the groves of mulberry at the edge of town? The silk industry has at last brought wealth to the city."

"What is that huge church?" Etienne pointed to an enormous white marble structure.

"That," said the driver proudly, "is our Duomo, our famous cathedral. Look at the top of each of those spires, and you will see a statue of a biblical or historical figure—135 of them."

"It's so elaborate!" exclaimed their mother.

"They've been working on it for over three hundred years. And it's not finished yet."

"It's truly magnificent," said Françoise. "I hope we can visit it sometime."

The driver turned onto the Via Padova. "The Marinelli villa is on this street. You can go to mass at the cathedral every Sunday if you wish."

Etienne checked his leather pouch and showed Françoise what was left—only a few coins of their depleted funds. When the coach pulled up to the gate of the Marinelli villa, he offered them as a small gratuity to the driver. The money had been just enough to cover their needs to this point.

They stepped down from the coach and looked up to the villa before them. "This is a palace!" exclaimed Etienne as the departing coach wheels clattered away over the cobblestones. "It has a red-tile roof like the other buildings, but look at all the pillars and those arched windows and the long, wide walkway up to the entrance."

"I love the gardens and fountains!" said Françoise with enthusiasm. "We will be surrounded by beauty—and another Marinelli family."

"Well, children, this is to be our home for a while," said their mother. "Let us enjoy what God has provided." She rang the summons bell.

After a few minutes, a servant, who said his name was Sergio, arrived. He was a boy not much older than Etienne.

"Buona sera, signora," he said. "Whom shall I announce is calling?"

"Please advise Signore and Signora Marinelli that the Chaplain family has arrived from France. Signore's brother, Pietro Marinelli, has sent us," said Françoise's mother in halting Italian. "They should have received a message."

Sergio looked puzzled. "Wait here, por favore." He disappeared into a side entrance and didn't return for nearly a half hour.

When he finally came back, he unlocked the gate and said, "You are to come to the servants' entrance. Follow me."

Shocked at this reception, they thought there must be some misunderstanding. "The message," said Françoise's mother. "Signore received it?"

"Sì. Signora is expecting you. But Signore Marinelli has been away on business for several weeks. I believe he is unaware that you were coming. This way, please."

⋙

They found the servants' quarters comfortable enough. Françoise and her mother shared a small room—more like a stall with a curtain drawn across the opening. Furnishings consisted of straw mattresses, a commode and wash basin, and a few hooks for hanging clothes. Etienne would bunk with three other boys, including Sergio, who had met them at the gate.

The chief house servant, Mira, a stout woman of Portuguese descent, helped settle them in and provided them with domestic garments—black with high white collars. Françoise gladly donned them, for they were not dissimilar to the simple Huguenot clothes they had burned. Their own clothing, altered at the house with Signora Isabella, could be laundered and reserved for Sundays. The other domestics showed them little curiosity, for apparently servants came and went rather often.

The next morning, Mira assigned Françoise and her mother various tasks and toiled alongside them. "I see you two have worked kitchens before. Most often I must waste my time teaching the new girls the simplest of routines," she said as they finished washing dishes from the morning meal. "I don't know what Signora Caterina means to do with you. She has not told me a thing. The boy most likely will be sent to a factory. We don't rightly need another stable hand."

"Is that where Etienne is this morning?" his mother asked. "He loves horses. That would really be a fine job for him."

Though puzzled they had been received as servants, Françoise went about her work cheerfully. After the long, tiresome journey, activity invigorated her.

That evening the two women prayed and sang psalms in their little chamber by candlelight. Françoise missed Etienne, off in his own quarters where he could not participate in the usual family worship. Mother and daughter prepared for bed and sat on their mattresses.

"I wonder if Signore Pietro knew we would be received as servants," mused Françoise. "I found much joy working beside Signora Isabella. She treated us as sisters."

"Yes, we grew to love her in such a short time. Here we have not so much as met our host and hostess—employers rather. Yet it is good of them to take us in. They have no reason to befriend us. And certainly we wish to work for our keep until we can find our own way."

"And, Mamma, I think of the Holy Scripture Paul wrote in

the Epistle to the Colossians: 'Whatsoever ye do, do it heartily as to the Lord, and not unto men.'"

"We must remember that as we go about our tasks," said her mother. "I do miss Etienne, though. At the supper tables tonight, he seemed to have made friends among the servant boys, Sergio in particular. They were all laughing and shoving each other as boys do. The women pay us little mind, though."

Her mother snuffed out the candle, and they lay down to continue their talk in the dark. "Françoise, we must find you a husband."

"What, Mamma?" said a startled Françoise. "I never think of such things. Guillaume is dead. I don't want to love another. You know yourself how great the pain of loss is."

"Yes, Daughter, but we must be practical. I have lived my life, and it was a good one, but it is all gone. I can accept whatever station in life befalls me. Now I live only to see you and precious Etienne find meaningful paths to happiness. For a woman, that path comes only through a good marriage. You are young, talented, and attractive. I am only saying we need to be thinking about your future."

"I suppose so, Mamma," she said with a sigh. *Stefano would have been a good choice.* She closed her eyes. *Will I ever see him again? 'Someday I will come to Milan,' he said, but Milan is so far away. How can he ever leave his farm?* She smiled at pleasant memories of him, turned her face to the wall, and fell asleep.

ᝍ

It was the third day, and still the Signora Caterina Marinelli had not met her guests. This morning Françoise and her mother were tidying the front salon where, on two of the walls, hung huge tapestries—a hunting scene and a pilgrimage to a church. They paused to admire some of the large oil paintings in elaborate gold frames—one of ladies dancing in the forest, signed by Botticelli, and two portraits by Raphael. "I have heard of Raphael," said Françoise, "but who is Botticelli?"

"Some Italian, I suppose," said her mother as she dusted the base of a marble column.

At that moment, Signora Caterina called them to a little alcove by the staircase. "Signora Elise and Signorina Françoise, do sit down. I am Signora Caterina Marinelli. A messenger brought this letter a week ago penned by my husband's brother, Pietro Marinelli," she said, looking over the letter in her hand. She was a full-figured woman with an aristocratic profile and heavy, dark eyebrows she raised and lowered like gestures.

"He does not say how he met you or why he is sending you to us. He says he has heard through mutual friends that I am 'in need of women's help and companionship.' He says you will be 'good company.' He mentions our acquaintance with the Grand Duke of Tuscany, who might be of some help, but I don't know that the man has ever helped anyone unless it was greatly to his advantage. Then Pietro goes on to say, 'The boy is a good worker and would be helpful with the horses.' So where did he find you, and why are you here?" Her eyebrows shot up. "I've really had no trouble in finding domestic servants."

Françoise noticed the servant role seemed ambiguous in the letter. Signore Pietro probably intended an arrangement more akin to what he himself had provided, but she would not protest.

Her mother answered as best she could in simple Italian sentences. "Our house burned down. My husband and three children died. We were destitute." Certainly Françoise did not expect her to reveal their full story.

"Signore Pietro is a good Christian man," added Françoise. "Civil war has come even to the countryside in France. He thought we could manage better here."

"If we could work for you until we can—"

"I see," said Signora Caterina. "My husband should be back from his business journey to Lyon, France, this night or on the morrow. He is in the silk trade. Probably he will want to place your son as an apprentice in one of our silk factories."

She lowered her eyebrows to a frown. "We have no need for

another stable boy. As for you, signora, Mira tells me you seem trustworthy to her. I would like to take you on as my personal servant and companion. Recently my maidservant left me to marry her swain. She had been with me for three years, since she was twelve. A sweet young thing, but I really prefer an older woman. Would that be satisfactory?"

The mother hesitated. Françoise bit her lip and watched her. This would be more of a commitment than working in the kitchen. La Rochelle had been a prosperous town, but few people ever kept servants. They simply helped their neighbors when necessary. No one lived in this kind of luxury. The social class system seemed strange, but she knew both she and her mother must earn their way somehow.

"Certainly," her mother said. "That will be satisfactory."

"And you, young lady—Françoise, is it?" said Signora Caterina. "You will marry soon, I presume. Just help Mira with whatever she tells you."

❧

Signore Matteo did, indeed, arrive home the next day and concurred in his wife's plans for the Chaplains. Françoise was delighted he spoke with her family in French. Everyone seemed happier when he was about. A large, jolly sort of fellow, he often sang and accompanied himself on the lute.

He discovered that Etienne could read and do arithmetic. "I will teach him all phases of the silk trade," he said, "but I especially will need him to keep ledgers when he is a little older." Etienne would stay at the factory dormitory during the week and spend Sundays with his family.

Françoise found plenty of work and threw herself into it wholeheartedly—"as to the Lord." But the other servant girls talked among themselves and ignored her presence. Each day she would look forward to the brief time with her mother in the evening, singing, praying, and talking. Françoise became even closer to her mother than before as they shared the events of the day more like sisters.

One day Signora Caterina asked her mother to move into a

chamber adjoining hers. She said she didn't wish to be so alone when her husband took his long business trips. When he was home, however, she would be free to return to her daughter's quarters. Without this time with her mother, Françoise felt isolated and lonely. Images of the tragic deaths of her loved ones haunted her at night and robbed her of sleep. She worked alone and rarely spoke all day beyond "Sì, Mira."

⁊

Two months passed. All three settled into their new roles. Françoise looked forward to Sunday each week when Etienne would be with them. Weather permitting, she and her brother would walk with the other servants to the Duomo, the huge marble cathedral on the piazza. Their mother would ride with Signora Caterina in the family carriage drawn by four white horses.

The chill of winter filled the villa. Grand fireplaces heated the Marinelli living quarters, but Françoise, along with the other servants, had to make do with heat from the kitchen fires. She was, however, provided with warmer clothing—gray woolen hosen and a cape.

Françoise's task today consisted of shaking out all the feather-beds over the back balcony. Signore Matteo Marinelli had arrived this morning from another trip, this time to Genoa, and Signora Caterina wanted everything fresh and clean for him. This afternoon Françoise would help with the washing.

Nearly numb with cold from exposure outdoors on the balcony, Françoise crept downstairs, intending to make herself a cup of hot herbal tea. The smell of a newly lit wood fire drew her to the front salon instead of the kitchen. There she found Signore Matteo poking at the logs in a giant fireplace. Startled that the master was there and building his own fire, she stopped and turned to leave.

"No, no, Françoise, come warm yourself," he said.

She came in and held her chilled fingers toward the fire.

"Caterina tells me you play the lute," he said, picking up the instrument he kept next to his favorite chair. "She says that is what your mother told her. Is that a fact?"

She turned toward him with a sad sort of smile and moved away from the blazing fire. "Well, yes, a little. My father had begun to teach me—"

"Before he died in the house fire. I am deeply sorry for your loss." He began to strum a French folksong. "I find playing the lute lifts the spirit."

As it was a familiar tune, Françoise began to hum along with the strumming. Soon they were singing together. "Here—you try it," he said and handed her the lute.

"I don't know if I can remember," she said. But she took the instrument, sat down on a brocaded footstool, and began to finger the strings. Soon a simple tune came to her from the past. She continued to strum and sing several ditties.

"My daughter used to play; then she lost interest. My wife and I both enjoyed hearing her. She's married now and lives in Rome with a family of her own. I hope some of my grandchildren will love music as I do," he said. "You may come here anytime to play my lute, whether or not I am in residence. Would you like that, Françoise?"

Françoise gasped with delight. "Indeed, I would like that very much. Thank you, signore. But now I must get back to my tasks." For a short pleasant while, she had forgotten her servant role.

&

Because Signore Matteo was home, Françoise's mother came back to her room for the night. With much enthusiasm, Françoise told of the joy she felt playing the lute again. "He is a most gracious and generous man, Mamma. He says I can play his lute anytime I wish—of course, that would be after my work is finished. He encourages me as Father did."

"He is pleased, no doubt, to find someone who shares his interest. I believe your access to music is a sign that better days are ahead, Françoise."

seven

Signore Matteo again was away in Lyon. One evening Françoise had finished her domestic chores following the supper. She had scrubbed the last table in the servants' eating room when she became aware of Mira standing in the doorway.

"Françoise, there is someone to see you," she said. "He is waiting in the front salon by the fireplace. You may go in."

He? Oh, Signore Matteo must be home unexpectedly. She wiped her hands and hung the cloth. This seemed unlikely as he had left only three weeks ago.

She stopped at the small broken mirror that hung by the kitchen doorway. Since working here, she seldom braided her long hair and wound it into a bun as in past times. Instead, she let it fall and bound it with a simple ribbon at the nape of her neck. She retied the pink ribbon and removed her apron. Signore Matteo always spoke to her more as a daughter than a servant; thus she wished not to appear as one. Whether it were he or not, she wanted to be presentable. She lit a candle and carried it with her.

In the dim light from the fireplace, she saw a man sitting in Signore Matteo's chair and assumed it was he. The man stood as she entered.

"Françoise," he said softly.

"Stefano?"

She set the candle on a stand, and without another word, they fell into each other's arms. Stefano held her closely, and she responded to his embrace. After a few moments, he looked into her eyes and brushed back the wisps of curls from her face. "You are beautiful, Françoise, and I love you," he whispered. "I never want to be long away from you again."

She turned her face up to him and closed her eyes. He accepted the invitation. As the kiss lingered, she sensed happiness—and a depth of emotion—surge through her.

Clearly she had heard his words but pulled away and said nothing in response to them. Instead of the usual footstool where she played the lute with Signore Matteo, tonight she chose a chair close to Stefano and leaned toward him, hand on chin. "I thought I would never see you again, Stefano. When did you get here? Why? Did anyone come with you? Tell me everything. How are your mother and father and brother?"

He laughed at her eagerness. "Did I not tell you I would come to you in Milan? I will tell you everything, and it is not all good news. But I am yet not ready. I just want to look at you and enjoy being near you." He leaned toward her and gently kissed her lips. "I will be staying here for a while. Uncle Matteo has all sorts of connections, even with Cosimo de' Medici, the Grand Duke of Tuscany, and he has assured me he can arrange a high-ranking apprenticeship, possibly in banking."

"When could you have seen your uncle? He has been away for nearly a month," she said with surprise.

He took her hand in his. "Uncle Matteo sent me a letter from Lyon, where he does business. It's a difficult story, but I will tell you everything. Not just yet, though. Mother is here with me—an answer to one of your questions. She is quite tired and distraught but in good health."

"Is she resting then? And why distraught?"

"Yes, she is probably sleeping. You know what a long trip it is. We arrived midafternoon. We had a lot of news to share with Aunt Caterina. Mother has reason to be distraught, but I will get to that. First, tell me about your journey here and how you are faring. I am annoyed that my aunt should treat you as a servant. We meant for you to be received as guests."

"It is really best this way. We find it hard to accept charity." She chatted away in French, telling him of all she could remember, beginning with the man dying of the plague at the port of Bordeaux and not stopping until their arrival at the gate of the villa. "My life here is not difficult, just very different from when we were in La Rochelle. It is not interesting to talk about. Except your uncle allows me to play his lute. He even encourages me to play when he is absent. It is bold of me to come into this magnificent hall and play the master's lute. I don't know what your aunt Caterina thinks about it. She never says anything, and even Mother has difficulty perceiving her intents. I try not to play except in the evenings after she has retired so as not to disturb her."

"She enjoys your music."

"How do you know that?"

He squeezed her hand. "Because she told me so. She opens her door at night and listens. Their daughter used to play the lute, you know."

"I know."

"Will you play and sing for me?" He handed her his uncle's lute.

"I have been composing music to go with the psalms we sing. Here is one I have been working on. It's Psalm 100." She hesitated, suddenly shy to sing in front of him. She moved to the stool where she was wont to play. "Tell me what you think."

His pleased expression encouraged her. After playing and singing several psalms, she paused. "Women, I'm told, are not capable of creativity, but composing music brings a bit of joy into my dull life. I composed both the lyrics and the music for this." She sang:

> *"Alone among people I do not know—*
> *Could they be friend; could they be foe?*
> *My Lord is with me; He guides me each day—*
> *He alone I trust to show me the way."*

"God has given you a most beautiful voice, Françoise, and a

talent for playing music. There is no harm in composing that I can see. Did you know there is a harpsichord in the family chapel? A priest used to come for private services when my cousin lived at home, but now my aunt and uncle go to the Duomo. Will you play for me every evening I am here?"

"No, I didn't know about the harpsichord, and, yes, I will play and sing for you whenever you like—whenever I have completed my tasks. But you know as well as I, Stefano, that it is not proper for us to be alone like this. Under normal circumstances—"

"These are not normal circumstances, Françoise," he said. He looked at her intently, then blurted out, "My father has been arrested. He is in prison in Lyon. Uncle Matteo heard about it and visited him there—brought him clothes and food. As he left, he met someone from our network going in to visit. It was to this man he gave the letter to bring to me in Bordeaux. It all happened soon after your departure."

"Oh, Stefano, was it because of us, because he harbored our family?"

"Not entirely. We helped many people. I am not even sure the militia knew about you specifically. We were part of a large underground network. The cache that my father kept in the barn was not entirely his money. People contributed who didn't want to risk contact with the refugees. He couldn't tell you that because everything had to be kept in total secrecy. That is one reason he told you not to repay him. We aided wounded government soldiers, too. Whomever God sent to us."

"I am so sorry, Stefano. Your father does only good. We owe him our lives. Will he have a fair trial? Did your uncle reveal his state of health in the letter?" Overcome with emotion, she put her hands over her face and wept.

"He is alive. That is all the letter said about his welfare. Uncle Matteo should be back here within a week. Perhaps he can tell us more." He stood and pulled her to him. "I remember another night when I held you weeping. That time it was for your family. Now it is for mine. That is all right; there is much to grieve over."

She sobbed, without control, until her body shook. He held her ever more closely. Finally, she quieted and pulled a handkerchief from her sleeve. She wiped her eyes. "I am so glad you are here, Stefano."

"So am I. Burdens are always lighter when two share them. Thank you for sharing mine." He kissed her eyelids. "We will have much time together in the days ahead. I must now bid you a good night." He handed her the candle she had brought with her and kissed her forehead. "Did you hear me say I love you, Françoise? Because I do. I love you with all my heart."

She sighed heavily and waited a few moments to respond.

"Yes, I heard what you said. Give me time, Stefano." Her mouth quivered, attempting a smile. "Good night."

She slipped away through the darkness, surrounded by the glow of her candle and the glow of Stefano's presence within her soul.

ও

For Françoise, the days following overflowed with happiness because Stefano was near, even when they were not together. Yet she grieved with both Stefano and his mother, Isabella, about his father in prison and prayed for his release.

From the day Françoise met Signora Caterina, she sensed the woman dismissed her as an unwanted and unnecessary servant who would soon marry and move on. Certainly she was less accepted and needed than her mother. For this reason, Françoise was surprised to learn from Stefano that Signora Caterina enjoyed hearing her sing and play the lute late at night. She showed favor to her nephew, Stefano, and perhaps as a courtesy to him now treated Françoise with more respect. Signora Caterina seemed a complex woman, difficult to guess her motives and feelings.

The day after Stefano arrived, she had called Françoise aside. "Under the circumstances, no longer consider yourself a servant here, but my guest. You do not need to wear the domestic garment, but wear the clothing you have made for Sundays."

"As you wish, signora," she had said. "But what do you want me to do?"

"It is time you begin sewing for your *cassone*."

"But, signora, I have no *cassone*!" Françoise's mouth hung open in utter disbelief.

"You will have one. My woodcarvers will begin on the chest today. We have bolts of fine silk from which you can make your garments, and I, personally, will show you how to embroider gold and silver thread onto the cloth." With a slight lift of her eyebrows, she turned and left Françoise wondering, *Under what circumstances? And why would a poor girl like me need a wedding chest?*

Signora Caterina did not release Françoise's mother from her position as personal maidservant and companion, because she claimed she had become irreplaceable. But she was allowed to make and wear her own clothing.

On many days, Signora Isabella and Françoise knitted or sewed by the fireplace in one of the smaller sitting rooms. Her mother joined them for short periods, and even Signora Caterina came occasionally. Signora Isabella told and retold the story of her husband's arrest, the dangers of the network in which they had involved themselves, and her fear of the future. Now, speaking in her native Italian, her words flowed.

All four women were seated around the fireplace in a small salon this cold February afternoon, doing needlework.

"I tried to convince Pietro that the network put our own lives in danger, but he always felt the Lord had called him to help any who came to us. How could I argue against God's call?" Signora Isabella was knitting a green wool scarf as she spoke.

"You could not have," said Françoise's mother. "In the end, my husband died for his beliefs."

"I wasn't home when they arrested him," continued Signora Isabella. "Stefano had taken me to my sister Josephine's in

Bordeaux. They try to keep strangers out of the city, but with the cooler weather, the plague had subsided. Besides, it never spread to the outskirts where she lived.

"Josephine remained angry at Pietro for becoming involved with the network. She blamed Stefano, as well, but I convinced her to allow him to stay. I thought of you, Elise, and how you had lost children as well as your husband. I wanted to keep one of mine with me, and my sister could not argue that point. Pietro and Giulio stayed behind. They had hired a manager, a young man named Gaston, to care for the farm. Then they planned to call on our network to arrange their transport to Geneva." The knitting needles flew faster as she continued her story.

"If they made it to Geneva, Giulio wanted eventually to go to Paris and become a student at the Sorbonne. That was always a distant dream of his. I pray he makes it. No one knows what became of him. They took Pietro from our house, but Giulio must have hidden. We heard news of the arrest right away, but we didn't know where they had taken him until the letter came from his brother, Matteo, several weeks later." She rolled up the incomplete scarf and tucked it into her bag.

"Matteo intended to visit Pietro again while in Lyon. Perhaps he will have news for you when he comes home," said Signora Caterina, laying down the shawl she had been working on.

Françoise had been quietly embroidering flowers on a silk bodice. She set it aside and said, "I will make us all a kettle of herb tea." The women concurred, and Françoise slipped off to the kitchens.

She turned to go back and ask Signora Caterina if she would care for sugar—as was the case on rare occasions. But she stopped short upon overhearing Signora Isabella whisper, "I don't believe she knows Stefano plans to marry her. She has said nothing to me. Elise, she does love him, does she not?"

"Of course she knows," said Signora Caterina before her

mother could answer. "I told her she could no longer work as a servant 'under the circumstances.' Why would she not know? They spent that first evening together in the salon, without a chaperone, and they see each other quite often. Why else would she be sewing this pretty little thing?" She held up the silk bodice. "She does lovely work."

Françoise's heart beat faster at the words she was hearing.

"No, she does not know," said her mother. "She would have told me had he mentioned marriage to her. I know she would."

"But Stefano came to both of us the afternoon you arrived, Isabella," pointed out Signora Caterina. "You had gone to lie down, exhausted as you were from traveling. But he said you had already consented. And, Elise, did you not consent for your daughter to marry him?"

Her mother spoke nothing for a moment, then finally said, "Yes, I did. We arrange such things differently in La Rochelle. Stefano is a fine young man, and I would be very proud for my daughter to be betrothed to him, but—"

"Of course, nothing official can be decided until Matteo gives his consent. He's the only male since Pietro. . . ," interjected Signora Caterina.

"She had a small dowry. My husband began an account for her at the age of one year," said her mother with some anguish in her voice. "It may have been confiscated."

"Why would—?" began Signora Caterina.

"Stefano is not concerned about her dowry," said Signora Isabella. "I believe he wants to be assured of Matteo's approval. And he will want to be the one to approach her. . . ."

Françoise hastened to the kitchen without hearing more, then returned minutes later carrying a tray of cups, a kettle, and a small pitcher of cream. Cheerily, she announced, "Tea for everyone."

eight

Before Stefano left Bordeaux, Gaston had delivered proceeds of the harvest to him; thus, he and his mother were presently in purse. To live among the merchant-banker class, he thought it wise to have fashionable outfits made for him. Aunt Caterina recommended her husband's tailor. He transformed easily from his recent past as a peasant farmer into a dashing aristocrat. He even grew a mustache and short, pointed beard. Though she teased him about it, Françoise pronounced it most handsome.

"And now you carry a dress sword, Stefano?" asked Françoise with a chuckle. "What a gentleman you have become." They had just entered the salon from opposite sides—a planned rendezvous.

"Do you like it, my dear?" he said in a mockingly arrogant tone. "I had it delivered to me this morning—to impress my ladylove."

"I am duly impressed, signore," she said. He held out the sword and let her run her fingers over the bejeweled and elaborately decorated scabbard. "You like your life here in the city of Milan better than in France, do you not, Stefano?"

"Let's go for a walk in the gardens. I will answer your question and any others. We have much to talk about," he said rather abruptly. "Go fetch your cape, and I will lay aside my sword."

Stefano waited as Françoise ascended the stairs to her new quarters, a small room on the second story, down the corridor from her mother's chamber. She soon returned wearing the gray cape he had seen her wear as a servant girl, over his mother's altered dress. She had taken to plaiting her hair again, wound in a bun, high on the top of her head. He thought the French style flattered her tall, slender figure.

He could hardly conceal his elation as he anticipated their time together and the words he would eventually say. He met her and took her hand. Together they walked down a long hallway to a side exit and through a portico to the garden paths.

"In the spring, flowers will bloom all along these alleyways," said Stefano, breathing in the fresh air. The day was unseasonably warm with sunshine and a cloudless blue sky. "Now to answer your question: I remember Milan as a child. We lived in a villa, much smaller than this, but a very fine home with grounds and a little garden where Giulio and I used to play. But it was a frightening time for a child. My father lost nearly everything, as you know. France and the Spanish Empire were fighting for control of this town. Now that has been settled, and we have our own rulers—but under Spain. Milan is a beautiful city. I enjoy the excitement, the festivals, and the wonderful art. I had forgotten about the great statues and paintings. Do you know of Leonardo da Vinci?"

"No, I do not know him," she said.

"He was a famous artist who lived for a while in Milan some fifty years ago. He painted a mural called *The Last Supper* on the wall inside a monastery right here in this city. Perhaps we can go see it together sometime. When I saw it as a boy, it seemed so huge and magnificent. I suppose it is still there."

"The only art I have seen is what's in your villa and in the Duomo," said Françoise. "Who are the people in the portraits in the front salon?"

"Those are my grandparents, my father and Uncle Matteo's parents, painted by another great artist by the name of Raphael. But I have strayed from answering your question. Do I like Milan or France better? The lifestyles are very different, and certainly this is a grander place. But I miss working out of doors, the smell of hay, the vineyards, milking the cows early in the morning. What do you think of Milan?"

"I think it a grand place, but it means nothing to me," said Françoise. "Frankly, my life here has been lonely. Until you came." She smiled up at him.

He took her hand and pulled her beside him on a marble bench with carved dolphins serving as armrests. "My life has been rather miserable and lonely also these past months. You were always in my heart. Now that you are with me, my heart sings with happiness. I will always love you, Françoise."

Stefano detected a shadow of sadness pass over her face that he could not interpret. The sweet togetherness evaporated at the mention of love.

"Do you love me, Françoise?"

"I admire you very much," she said, looking down at her hands twisting her handkerchief. "I am happiest when I am with you, but. . ."

"But what? Françoise, you can tell me whatever is in your heart."

"I don't know if I can ever love you—not completely, not wholeheartedly as one should. I loved someone once. . . ."

"And so you still love his memory?"

"No, no, that is not it."

Stefano put his arm around her shoulders and drew her to him. But he felt her body stiffen and draw back. He released her and withdrew his arm.

"Then I don't understand," he said.

She looked out over the city, past the distant spires of the Duomo, past him. "I have lost so many members of my family that I love. It's as if part of me has been torn away, and the part that remains, that wants to love you, cannot."

"Time will heal your hurts, Françoise. Think about your future and forget your past." He heard his words sound argumentative and hollow, not at all as he intended.

She continued to stare out into space and remained silent.

In a desperate effort to bring her back to him, he said, "Françoise, I plan to ask Uncle Matteo to arrange our marriage—since our fathers cannot do that for us. But our mothers have consented. I love you deeply and, in time, I believe you will love me."

She turned and looked at him, but he could not read what lay behind those beautiful, long-lashed eyes.

"Will you be my wife, Françoise?" Stefano struggled to bridge the distance between them.

"Yes, Stefano, I will," she said and stood to go.

To Stefano, her words sounded determined—and forced. Where was the joy he'd expected?

He took her hand, and they walked back to the villa. He believed she was concealing a sadness he could not reach. He had blundered his proposal, a moment he had planned would bring immense happiness. There could be no joy in a yes given reluctantly. Was there something more—beyond the family deaths—that built a wall around her heart? Did she still love the suitor who died? Did he compare unfavorably with that other?

≥≥

When a forerunner brought the alert to Stefano that his uncle Matteo's entourage had crossed the Ticino River and would arrive by nightfall, excitement spread throughout the villa. Stefano wandered aimlessly through the halls, pondering still more questions: Could there be good news about his father's fate? Would he know the whereabouts of Giulio? Would his uncle agree to his betrothal to an indigent French girl, a former servant of his own household? Was Queen Catherine de' Medici still controlling France through her young son, King Charles? Had civil war subsided there?

Stefano's anticipation grew as the day wore on. Servants bustled about preparing a feast of veal and pheasant, pasta and cheeses, and the best of wine from the cellars.

≥≥

Finally, Uncle Matteo arrived at his villa with young Etienne, whom he had picked up at his major factory. The families gathered around them in the salon with welcoming words. He explained he had left instructions with his overseers for building a newly invented waterwheel that would speed silk production.

Though Stefano would have liked to pursue talk of this new invention, he knew Françoise and her mother had not seen Etienne in some time, as the weekly visits had dwindled to once a month. He stood aside as they smothered the boy with hugs and kisses until his cheeks reddened. Though taller and thinner, he appeared in good health. He said he was spending more time keeping ledgers now, which pleased his interests.

But he had one complaint. "The rats bother us at night. They are fat and ugly, and since our straw mats lie on the floor, they come right up to us. Once I awoke and saw a rat's hideous eyes staring at me—only a hand's span from my face."

His mother and sister gasped and covered their faces with their hands.

Stefano saw the grin on Etienne's face and chuckled. "You shouldn't repulse the ladies with such tales."

At dinner, all disgusting talk of rats ceased. The focus turned entirely on Uncle Matteo and the news he might share. The servant girls hovered around the table of seven, attending to every need, until Stefano shooed them away. He was less hungry for food than for his uncle's information.

"I am afraid the war rages on in France," continued Uncle Matteo at the head of the table. "Poor King Charles. They say he languishes in remorse over the massacre in Paris but is powerless to challenge his mother's wishes."

"The French never accepted Queen Catherine because she's Italian," said Stefano, refusing a second helping of pasta. "They blame her for much of the unrest."

"And rightly so, I think," said his uncle as he motioned to a servant to fill his glass. "The people are tired of strife."

Stefano noticed the anxious expression on his mother's blanched face. He guessed she dreaded news that his uncle was holding back. At that moment, Uncle Matteo glanced at Stefano's mother and indicated to the servants that they should clear the dishes from the table and leave them in private.

Uncle Matteo lowered his voice and leaned toward his sister-in-law at his left. "I have no word on Giulio, Isabella, and I made three trips to the prison in an attempt to visit Pietro. Each time I left food and drink with the guards, who eagerly accepted it."

"He is dead, isn't he?" said his sister-in-law in a scarcely audible voice. "My husband is dead." Stefano took his mother's hand, but she closed her eyes and remained silent.

"Go on, Uncle—we will hear you out," said Stefano.

"Yes, Isabella, Pietro is dead," said Uncle Matteo. "I am sorry to bring you this news. I went back a fourth time the day before I left Lyon. Just as my servant and I stepped from my carriage, I saw the man I had met before from the network walk by. He is the one who carried my letter to you, Stefano. I asked him if he was there to visit Pietro. He told me no, it was for another. 'Pietro died over two weeks ago,' he told me, and they even refused to give him his body. He could tell me nothing about how he died. I tried in vain to gather information from authorities, but they would only confirm his death."

The group remained quiet for several minutes. Françoise, who sat on the other side of Stefano, laid her hand over his. He sat thus linked between the two women he most loved but felt little comfort.

"We will have a service of memorial for Pietro in our family chapel tomorrow, Sunday afternoon. I have already spoken to the priest who used to come for our private family worship," said Uncle Matteo.

"That is good," said Aunt Caterina.

Signora Elise and Aunt Caterina helped his mother to her room. When they returned, Signora Elise, with tears in her eyes, told Stefano, "We offered to stay and pray with her, but she dismissed us, saying she wished to be alone with God and memories of her dear husband."

&

Nearly a week passed without Stefano spending any time alone with Françoise. Their relationship became one of polite affection, as Stefano felt uneasy over their unfinished conversation. His uncle Matteo had requested that Françoise play the harpsichord at the memorial service. His mother asked that she and Etienne sing Psalm 61 as they had done before departure from their home: "When my heart is overwhelmed, lead me to the rock that is higher than I." She said her husband enjoyed hearing their manner of worship.

Stefano's mother remained dry-eyed through the service, but tears ran down his face as he listened to Françoise's sad but beautiful voice. Not only had he lost his father, but he feared the angelic Françoise was lost to him, as well. Her assent to his proposal felt more like a refusal.

&

Days later, as he sat reading in the library, his heart sang when he looked up and saw Françoise standing in the doorway.

"So this is where you spend your time," she said. "May I disturb you?"

"I am disturbed only by your absence, Françoise. Please come and sit beside me." She took a place beside him on a double bench upholstered in burgundy velvet.

"Mother says I must talk to you. But not even she knows what I struggle with most. Please do not mention to her what I am about to say."

"Surely you know you can trust me, Françoise." He thought she flinched at the word *trust*.

"Do not think me unkind or ungrateful for all your family has risked for us. You have only been kind and good." She stared for a long time into the smoldering coals of the fireplace and pulled her shawl about her. Finally, she sighed. "I can never again trust my heart to another man."

"Françoise, look at me." He turned her face toward him. "I am the man who loves you with all my heart, my whole being. There is nothing I would not do to protect you. I would never say or do anything that would harm you." He put his arms around her and tenderly kissed her lips, then took her hand. "Tell me with what you struggle."

Françoise relaxed in his arms but remained passive.

"Françoise, I apologize for the words I said to you in the garden. I told you to forget the tragedies of your past and look to the future. Now that I have lost my dear father, I know that one's past will always be a part of that person. To love another, one must embrace the past also. I know I will always carry with me terrible images of how my father died—whether he was executed or starved. I will never know. I understand better now the sorrows you carry with you. But—"

She lifted her face to his and yielded to his embrace. He held her close and kissed her—as ardently as he dared. She pulled away and moved to a nearby chair.

"I will tell you, Stefano," she said, looking into his eyes. "You know that my suitor was shot when the soldiers raided our house. I loved Guillaume. I thought him good and kind. My father and he were in discussions about our betrothal. In La Rochelle, no one trusted anyone anymore. Even the Huguenots mistrusted each other. Spies were everywhere. We never knew who killed my older brother in a street fight."

"You've never told me before how he died. Go on."

"Well, I trusted Guillaume with all my heart. He practiced his faith in the same manner as we. But he held to the more radical practices of the iconoclasts. I thought nothing about his leanings, as love blinded me." Tears began to trickle down her cheeks. She wiped them with her handkerchief. "I trusted him with the same story I told you about my father and brother removing the harpsichord from the church. I never told another person, besides Guillaume, until I told you that night at your aunt Josephine's. I realized then as I told the story aloud that what I suspected was surely true."

"And what was that?"

"Guillaume had told the authorities. I am now sure of it. Thus he brought destruction on our family—and unwittingly on himself. I have told you everything now. It is the pain of his betrayal of my trust that I cannot get past. Somehow in my mind I associate romantic love with betrayal. I don't understand that myself. It's as though my heart loves so far, then stops loving. As if a wall is there. . .perhaps a protection against facing such a deep hurt again."

"Françoise, do you love me enough to be my wife?"

"I have told you all the secrets of my heart. I consent to be your wife. I want to share your bed, bear your children, and be loyal to you."

"But can you love me unreservedly?"

"No, Stefano, I don't believe I can. Please give me time to heal." She looked pleadingly at him. "I wish to give you more, but this is all I can offer now."

Stefano stared out the library window and pondered his dilemma. Finally, he got up and walked to the chair where she was sitting. She stood as he took her hand. "Then I will tell Uncle Matteo not to arrange for the *impalmare* ceremony. Let us postpone our betrothal until you are sure. But I will love no other unless you turn me away."

"I will not turn you away, Stefano. Thank you for giving me time."

nine

Stefano noticed that his mother and Françoise's, the two widows, spent a great deal of time together sharing their grief—when Signora Elise was not serving his aunt Caterina. When he found the three women together in the salon, he invited his uncle to come in, for he had something to say.

"The betrothal will be postponed for now." He gave no reason, but they agreed that was best during the mourning period for his father.

When the women left to go their separate ways, his uncle Matteo asked for a word with Stefano. They stood looking out the tall window toward the formal gardens of clipped hedges and slender cedars.

"Yes, Uncle Matteo?"

"Young man, though the betrothal is postponed, it is not too soon to launch your career."

Uncle Matteo stood with his arms crossed and looked his nephew over. "You recall I promised to help in this regard in the Bordeaux letter."

"Yes, I know, and I am ready, Uncle." In spite of the grief over his father's recent death and the uncertainty of his love relationship, he knew the importance of finding gainful work.

"I have sent word among my connections in high places that I have a brilliant nephew, highly gifted in mathematics, knowledgeable in art and literature, who speaks not only Italian but French, as well—for their foreign clients. At present, he is available to present himself as apprentice banker. He would be a valuable asset to whichever bank wins his favor."

"And which nephew would that be, Uncle Matteo?" He laughed at what he perceived as an inflated description of himself.

"I've not said a word of untruth, Stefano," his uncle said with a pat on his back. "I've added that your integrity is beyond reproach—which in the banking business is a rarity. Besides, with your new beard and dress sword, you look the part. The Sforza Bank here in Milan and the Medici in Florence will be vying for your talents. In the meantime, continue to study the books I have suggested to you."

⁂

Within a few days, Mira notified Stefano that Almeni—the personal servant of Cosimo de' Medici, Grand Duke of Tuscany—awaited with his uncle in the reception room. If this concerned his career, no higher personage could show him interest. He had hoped to hear from a representative of one of the banks, but the grand duke not only owned the Medici Bank, he ruled all of Tuscany like a king. Only Philip of Spain was greater.

Much to his surprise when he entered the reception room, he saw Françoise and his aunt Caterina sitting at the round table as well as his uncle and Almeni.

Almeni stood to shake the hand of Stefano. "You must be the talented nephew. I saw the ladies in the hallway and asked them to come in. I assume you have no objection, signore."

"None whatsoever, signore."

Stefano had heard that because Almeni was well educated and respected, the duke often sought his advice, considering him a counselor as well as a servant. Thus Stefano and his uncle deferred to him as a superior.

Almeni handed a folded parchment to Uncle Matteo. "This, signore," he said, "is an invitation for you, your wife, and your nephew to share in a gala dinner party at the grand duke's country villa on the outskirts of town one week from today. You will arrive at six of the clock for entertainment preceding dinner. Dancing will follow the meal. Two other young men and their parents have also received invitations." Uncle Matteo unfolded the parchment and read the information that had just been spoken to him.

"Please tell the grand duke we are pleased to accept his kind invitation," he said, then looked to the family members. "Even with this household still in mourning, I do not feel it inappropriate to accept this opportunity." They nodded agreement.

"The duke will be in residence for a few weeks to hunt and fish along the Ticino River and at Lake Maggiore before returning to Tuscany. And, humph, if I may ask," said Almeni, glancing toward Françoise, "is the young lady perchance betrothed to Stefano?"

"Well, at the moment, no, she is not," stated Uncle Matteo.

"Good, very good," he said. "I will see if I may gain an invitation for her, as well. I will relay your acceptance to my master."

Stefano wondered what Almeni meant by "good." Why would the duke be more likely to issue her an invitation if she were *not* betrothed to him?

At any rate, her invitation arrived the following day by a lesser servant. Françoise appeared more comfortable around Stefano now that the pressure of betrothal was lifted. She even told him she anticipated with pleasure attending a social function with him for the first time.

❧

The following day, Mira came to Françoise's room to inform her that Stefano requested a word with her. Laying aside the silk fabric Signora Caterina had given her to fashion a dress, she hastened to the landing and saw him waiting at the bottom of the grand staircase. She descended with a quizzical expression on her face. "Yes, what is it, Stefano?"

"I have a gift for you. I hope you do not mind." He seemed so ill at ease that Françoise forgave him for whatever indiscretion this might be. "I purchased it for you. . .for our betrothal. But I thought you might like to wear it for this occasion." His face flushed as he handed her a plain little box.

She opened it and gasped with delight. A short string of pearls lay in crushed velvet. "They are beautiful!" she said, lacing them through her fingers.

"As are you, my dear," said Stefano with a smile.

"I don't deserve such a gift, but I accept it nonetheless," she said, fastening the strand around her neck. "Your aunt Caterina offered to loan me a piece of jewelry for the evening, but now I have something of my own." Color rose to her cheeks, and she fingered the beads at her throat. "Thank you, Stefano." She kissed his cheek and ascended the staircase. Near the top, she turned and smiled at him before hurrying on.

She continued work on the formal dress she had been making for the upcoming occasion. Signora Caterina helped her add a collar that stood up in back to reflect the fashion in Florence.

&

Stefano spent his time studying his uncle's books: *Banking Practices of the Medici* and *Florentine Statues of Michelangelo*. Many of the artist's sculptures had been commissioned by the Medici family and thus would make for better conversation than spring planting and the birthing of calves.

&

Françoise sat next to Stefano and across from Signore Matteo and Signora Caterina in their gilded coach, pulled by fine white horses. She felt as fashionably attired as the Marinellis in her newly finished dress. The bodice revealed an inset of embroidered beige silk overlaid with blue velvet, the waist pointing down in front. The full skirt continued in blue velvet, the ample sleeves and collar in silk. Her cape was of fine, white wool. And, of course, around her bare neck she wore the single strand of pearls Stefano had given her.

Stefano was dressed in black save for his white silk shirt and brocaded doublet. His breeches, hosen, cape, and soft-leather boots were all in fashionable black as well as the hat with brim upturned on one side. Signore Matteo was similarly attired, and his wife wore dark green velvet and silk.

As they approached the villa, Françoise listened intently as Signore Matteo more fully enlightened them about their host. "You will find the grand duke Cosimo a handsome man who appears younger than his fifty-some years. His wife,

Eleonora, whom he adored and who advised him on everything from politics to finance, died ten years ago. Of his eight children, only two remain alive. Four succumbed in their teens to various illnesses, and his favorite daughter was tragically murdered by her husband. He himself fears assassination, and, indeed, many attempts have been made on his life."

"How does he rule all of Tuscany with such a burden of sorrow?" Françoise wondered aloud.

"In fact, his interest in the family banking business has lagged," said Signora Matteo. "In the past year, the Medici Banks have lost many of their most essential staff to the Sforzas, to death, or to retirement. This explains his eagerness to raise up personally the best replacements. Thus, an opportune moment awaits you, Stefano."

&

For a country house used only a few times a year as a retreat, it was splendidly furnished and staffed. An enormous portrait of Cosimo himself, by the gifted artist Bronzino, hung over the fireplace in the ballroom. Other oil portraits of his wife and children and various members of the Medici family were scattered throughout.

For only ten guests, Françoise thought the entertainment seemed extravagant: jugglers, acrobats, dancers, and musicians. When the performing troops had made their exits, Cosimo asked that Signore Matteo play the lute to accompany the guests in singing. He obliged with a slight bow. Because Françoise had sung before with him, she knew much of what he played and sang in full voice.

Cosimo sat nearby and commented, "Signorina Françoise, what a lovely voice you have."

"Grazie, your highness," she said shyly.

"The lady also plays the lute and harpsichord," said Signore Matteo.

"Ah, then please favor us with a number on the harpsichord, my lovely lady, before we retire to the dining hall," said Cosimo, apparently delighted with the information.

"But—," she protested, as she felt her face flush crimson, "I know only psalms or compositions of my own making." She felt trapped. No one could refuse the Grand Duke of Tuscany.

"Psalms?" he laughed. "No others but French Huguenots sing psalms. And that without instrument."

Not uttering another word, Françoise got up and walked to the elaborately carved and gilded harpsichord. She sat and touched the keyboard. With trembling and perspiring hands, she attempted to play. Alas, it was all wrong. She stumbled with the unfamiliar instrument. The guests remained politely silent.

Françoise paused, breathed deeply, whispered a prayer, and launched, with some measure of confidence, into Psalm 100. She sang, "Make a joyful noise unto the Lord."

The guests applauded. Cosimo stood and shouted, "Bravo! Bravo for a woman who can play and sing like the angels in heaven. And who defies all logic by composing." Following his lead, the guests stood and applauded again.

With downcast eyes and still flushed, Françoise made her way back to Stefano, who reached to take her hand. Cosimo, however, intercepted it and tucked her arm under his. Together they headed toward the dining hall. All the guests followed.

"I award you the honor of sitting on my right side tonight, Signorina Françoise," Cosimo said.

Stefano sat with his aunt and uncle to the left of their host at the head of the table. The other guests found their places. The sumptuous meal consisted of several courses. Cosimo bragged about the trout he had caught himself on an early-morning fishing trip. Each person made a comment in praise of his skill in fishing. While eating, the duke briefly interviewed each young man and his family.

After dinner, they retired to the ballroom. The musicians struck up the dance music. Cosimo was deep in conversation with one of the other candidate's mothers. Thus he led the woman to the floor as his partner. Stefano and Françoise giggled like children as they positioned themselves—his hand on her waist, hers on his shoulder, left hands together. Stefano told her he had danced only to the folk music at local festivals. Françoise had never had occasion to dance in the religious community of La Rochelle. But her awkwardness soon gave way to the flow of the music and the joy of moving as one in this opulent ballroom. Françoise whispered to Stefano that she was happy to be free from Cosimo's attentions.

"The duke enjoys the company of beautiful young women, but they say he will never remarry," said Stefano. "Though he is attracted to you tonight, show him no favor, and he will forget you tomorrow."

"I do have sympathy for the man," said Françoise. "All those deaths in his family. I will try to be kind to him."

"Show him no favor—"

At that moment, Cosimo took her wrist and whisked her out of Stefano's arms. She recoiled at his touch. His hands were soft like dough, not like the rough calloused ones she cared for. The large man held her close, with his black-bearded cheek against hers. *I just wish this evening to end,* she thought.

"I want to spend time alone with you, my sweet," he whispered in her ear. She didn't know how to respond, so she said nothing. When the music became louder and livelier, he waltzed her behind three pillars clustered together. He pressed his hand against her waist and pulled her to him, then kissed her on the mouth. "I'll send for you someday soon," he whispered.

Stunned and repulsed by this sudden act, she paid little attention to his words, thinking only of escape.

As they emerged from behind the pillars, he pulled back, dancing with a good distance between them, and began talking loudly about the Uffizi Palace he had just built in Florence. "And now, my lovely Françoise, I must leave you to talk business matters." He released her to a chair next to the parents of one of the young men. A servant brought them cool drinks and dried figs. Though Françoise had eaten little at dinner, she refused the offerings. The loathsome experience with Cosimo left her trembling and feeling nauseous.

"You have a beautiful voice, signorina," said the lady beside her.

"Thank you, signora."

"Where did you learn to play the harpsichord?" inquired the man.

Françoise looked out over the dance floor and saw three women who had not been present before. They appeared quite young, dressed in flowing silks, and were dancing with the three young men—including Stefano.

"Thank you, signore," she said, having forgotten his question. She saw Cosimo, who was already conversing with Matteo, motion to Stefano to join them.

❧

On the way home in the carriage, Françoise learned that Cosimo had chosen only Stefano from the three candidates to apprentice at the main Medici Bank, headquartered in Florence. Signore Matteo and Stefano immediately began preparations the next day as Stefano was to report to the Florentine bank as soon as possible. Signore Matteo needed to tend to business alliances there anyway. Thus, he would accompany Stefano and assign him a personal servant for the trip as well as bring his own staff. Françoise began to miss him long before his departure, so preoccupied was he in his own affairs.

Following an evening meal as both tarried at the table, Stefano told Françoise, "It is only a few days' journey to Florence. I will send you a long letter with Uncle Matteo. This is a fine opportunity for me, for both of us, really. My proposal is still open to you, and my love will remain steadfast."

Visions of that other girl dancing and laughing in Stefano's arms flashed across her mind. *Will he forget me and find another who can love him more completely?*

But, trying to hide her concern, she said, "I know, Stefano. I wish you well in Florence."

Within a week he was gone. The three carriages left before sunrise. Françoise rose early enough to bid him farewell, but with the rush to be on their way and with so many people present, they had no time for tender moments. She could tell his mind had already left for the enticing city of great art, palaces, prestige, and financial ventures. From his heart, he only paused to say, "I will come to see you in early summer. Good-bye, my love."

"God be with you, Stefano."

No sooner had the carriages disappeared between rows of little shops than Signora Caterina called Françoise inside. Everyone else had returned to their morning activities. The two women stood just inside the entryway.

"You place me in a difficult dilemma," Signora Caterina said, not looking directly at her. "You have refused my nephew's offer of marriage, which most any girl in Italy or France would have snatched in a moment."

"Postponed," she offered limply.

"Not eagerly accepted, I would say. Whatever the case, Stefano will find a bride quickly enough in Florentine society. This new idea of allowing young people to have a say in their marriage choice will lead to the breakdown of society, if you ask me. My dilemma is what to do with you. I can no longer keep you as a guest since you are not betrothed to Stefano. Nor can I return you to a servant status—Matteo would not agree to that. Come sit down, and I will tell you the plans we have made for you."

"Was Stefano consulted?"

"No. His mind was rightly set on his new adventure. I'm sure he never thought of the position he left us in," Signora Caterina said with an exasperated lift of her eyebrows.

Françoise followed her into the front salon, where they took places before the grand fireplace. A chill hung in the air as no fire was lit.

"Some friends of ours, Lucrezia and Ferdinando Maffei, have been searching for a governess and tutor for their young children. They have two, a boy and a girl. I will provide a carriage to transport you and the belongings you have accumulated to their house. That includes the *cassone* and all you have placed therein."

"Thank you for your generosity, Signora Caterina," she said mechanically. "Does my mother know I am to leave?"

"I told her this morning as she dressed me," said Signora Caterina. "She believes this is for the best. Her only request was that you be allowed to return on the Sundays Etienne is here. Because your mother is very important to me, I have favored her by granting this request. You will begin your new duties Monday, the day following tomorrow." With that, Signora Caterina got up and left Françoise sitting alone to contemplate her future.

ten

Far away in Florence, Stefano settled into a large boarding-house room on Via delle Oche, not far from the bank where he would work. His pay of thirty florins for the first year was generous for his position, but out of that he had to pay his room and board and dress in a manner befitting his new class.

His immediate supervisor and teacher was a cousin of Cosimo's, Alessandro de' Medici. A small, hunched man with skinny fingers and a sharp nose, he taught Stefano the rudiments of banking as though he were divulging secrets. He spoke in a low tone, his beady eyes darting back and forth, and he punctuated each point with "You must always remember this, my son."

Stefano accepted the "my son" part as an attempt at affection, though nothing else about him offered friendship. He learned quickly and respected the man for his knowledge. The two other young men directly under Alessandro's care, however, mocked him in private. They had worked under him for six months or more and were beginning to act cocksure in their positions. Diego hailed from Madrid, valuable to the company for his Spanish heritage. Luigi claimed a distant tie to the Medici family, though he lacked its alleged brilliance.

"As young bankers, you will need to know much more than our system of double-entry bookkeeping and law," lectured Alessandro one afternoon as the three stood at their tall desks. "We are the financiers who create and circulate the wealth in Europe and, to a lesser extent, in the Orient. Crowned heads borrow from our banks to support their lavish lifestyles and finance their wars."

By working for the bank that loans them money, that puts me in the position of helping to support the government of France—the government that took the lives of Françoise's loved ones and my own dear father, thought Stefano with a twinge of guilt.

"We facilitate the flow of commissions from patrons—of which the Medici are chief—to artists, sculptors, architects, and aristocratic merchants. You need to be able to converse knowledgeably with our clients. Therefore, Stefano, you are to read this book, *Lives of the Painters*, which the other two have already read." As Alessandro handed him his assignment, Stefano was sure he detected Diego and Luigi exchanging a sneer behind the master's back.

"We have been invited to tour the art collections at the Palazzo Uffizi." Alessandro lowered his voice to emphasize the rare privilege they had been afforded. "The grand duke is still vacationing in Milan and thus will not be in residence, but this will be an important part of your education. Though it is but a short distance, we will all go by coach Monday morning."

With class dismissed, the three apprentices headed for a favorite nearby tavern, the Blue Goose, to relax and discuss the day's lessons. "You'll find that book boring, my friend," said Luigi. "Those artists would never have become famous without my family's help. I skipped most of it."

"Old Alessandro will quiz us on it as we view the works in the palace," said Diego. He took the book from Stefano and thumbed through it. "Who knows who painted the *Primavera*?"

"The same fellow who did *The Birth of Venus*. But who cares?" said Luigi.

"That would be Botticelli," said Stefano. "My uncle has a smaller painting by him. It's similar to the *Primavera*."

"Well, aren't you the smart one!" said Luigi. "Since you know so much, I'll just keep this little book over Sunday." He snatched it from Diego.

Stefano ignored the remark. He ordered beverages for all of them and paid the waitress. "Why don't both of you come to my room Sunday afternoon, and we'll study the painters together? We can test each other and really impress old Alessandro."

This was the first time Stefano had used "old" in reference to their master, but he felt it important to ingratiate himself to the others. They could easily subvert his training. Fortunately, his assertive suggestion to study together gained back the necessary book.

੨ⱥ

The state coach stopped in front of the Vecchio Palace, which stood adjacent to the Uffizi. "We will make a brief stop here to examine the famous statuary. When the grand duke lived here, he commissioned these statues not only for himself to enjoy, but all of Florence—and dignitaries from around the world," said Alessandro, alighting from the coach. The young men quickly followed. "Let us first study the celebrated Neptune fountain here in the piazza."

From there the group moved to the raised stone platform that ran the length of the façade. The master lectured and questioned his pupils as they strolled by the statues, stopping to admire his favorites: Florence's heraldic lion bearing the city's arms, Donatello's bronze *Judith and Holofernes*, and, last of all, Michelangelo's oversized *David*. "The sculptor released this magnificent human form from a single giant piece of marble—in less than two years!"

Stefano, truly amazed, subdued his praise and answered only questions posed directly to him or left unanswered by the others. He felt he needed the acceptance of his peers. Soon they progressed to the paintings hung four high in the grand galleries of the Uffizi, including works by Leonardo da Vinci, Raphael, Cellini, Caravaggio, and one by Michelangelo—a round panel with a touching rendition of *The Holy Family*.

Back outside, while they awaited the arrival of the state coach for their return, Alessandro pointed his skinny finger to the covered passageway that spanned the Arno River, connecting the Uffizi to the much larger and even more elaborate Palazzo Pitti on the other side. "Our grand duke Cosimo did not wish to be soaked by rain in crossing over from one palace to the other. Those little shops hanging along both sides of the bridge were already here, but he dismissed those merchants and replaced them with jewelers. I hope we can visit the Pitti someday."

Riding back in the coach after a long day of rigorous mental activity, Stefano gazed out at the city and marveled at the beauty his eyes had beheld. He thought of Françoise and how he would love for her to see these wonders with him. He felt ashamed that he had not thought of her more often and had neglected to pray for her welfare. He felt his faith faltering, caught up as he was in the splendor of his new life. He resolved to pray more and visit the Duomo on Sunday. Though he lived practically in its huge shadow, he had not so much as entered the cathedral for prayer.

In the coach, Alessandro droned on about the wonderful places they would visit another time: the bronze doors of the baptistery by Ghiberti, Brunelleschi's majestic cupola that towered over the city, the newly opened biblioteca that housed a prized collection of Medici books and manuscripts.

Luigi and Diego soon lost interest. They whispered about their rendezvous with some ladies of the evening. Diego jabbed his elbow into Stefano's ribs. "Want to come?"

Stefano raised his eyebrows and darted his eyes toward Alessandro as if to indicate they should talk of such things later. The coach soon pulled up to the boardinghouse the three shared on Via delle Oche. They all thanked the master for his "wonderful lectures" and voiced their appreciation for the "rare opportunity" he had so graciously provided.

No sooner had the coach carried away the master than Diego and Luigi burst into loud guffaws. "He's half deaf, you fool," said Diego. "Haven't you noticed? Besides, when he's enraptured about the wonders of Florence, he doesn't even notice us. So do you want to spend the night with some ladies or not?"

"Thank you for inviting me, but truly I have pressing work

to do tonight," he said with a handshake to each.

"What could be more pressing—?"

"Ah, come on, Diego—leave the man alone."

The two ambled down the street toward the amusement they sought. Stefano climbed the steps to his room. *I should have said my steadfast love was promised to another,* he thought.

ཟ

Françoise felt more at ease in the Maffei household than with Signora Caterina. Both Lucrezia and Ferdinando commended her efforts with their children. Like Signore Matteo, Ferdinando's business often took him away from his family. He owned a mule train, which transported Milanese silk to Florence, where he purchased bolts of finished wool. On the return trip, he passed through Genoa and sold his products along the way.

Though much smaller than the Marinelli villa, the Maffei dwelling was ample and tastefully furnished. An enclosed garden in the back allowed space for the children to play or do their lessons on warmer days. But Françoise felt isolated from the household and abandoned by Stefano, leaving her sad and lonely.

She suffered not only from the unhealed wounds in her heart, but also from allowing Stefano to slip away without betrothal. Though she missed him terribly, she struggled with committed love and worried that Stefano would stop loving her.

Her unwavering faith in God brought her only comfort. Every morning she knelt beside her bed and prayed. She asked blessings and protection for Stefano. And also for her mother and brother. Her own future, she believed, lay in God's hands, and she trusted Him to show her the way she should go. As she no longer had access to lute or harpsichord, she would softly sing one of her favorite psalms.

In the children's study room, Françoise sat across a table from nine-year-old Maria and her seven-year-old brother, Luca. She had devised a game for them to practice addition and subtraction on their father's ancient abacus. This was a new device to her, but she mastered the rudiments quickly enough to teach the children. Neither child had the benefit of formal education before Françoise became their governess, but they seemed delighted in their response to her. They now competed to be first with the correct answer.

"Ninety-nine minus thirty-two." Françoise touched her sleeve and fingered the letter she had stuffed there. Only a few minutes before, Lucrezia Maffei had brought it to her. "Signore Matteo has just sent this by his servant, Sergio. You may read it later," she had said. *It can only be from Stefano....*

"Fifty-seven!" shouted Luca.

"Yes, very good," said Françoise distractedly.

"No, it's not," said Maria. "It's *sixty*-seven. I'm right, am I not, signorina?"

"Yes, Maria. It is sixty-seven. That's eleven right for you and nine for Luca. You are both doing very well. And quick, too."

Before Luca could pout, a maid arrived to announce, "Time to come have something to eat, children."

As her charges scampered off to the kitchen, Françoise rushed to her room, pulled the letter from her sleeve, and threw herself prone across her bed. With her hands over her face, she lay there a few moments and wondered about the message she was going to read. *Was I wrong to want more time? Maybe I should have said the words of love and trust I did not honestly feel. Has he found another to love in Florence—like Signora Caterina said? What I do know is that I miss him more than I expected.* Her fingers trembled, and her heart raced as she untied the ribbon and broke the seal. *Three pages. He wrote me three full pages!*

My dearest Françoise,
    My life has changed so very much since I came to Florence. The city is much larger than Milan and full of palaces, fountains, and wonderful works of art. I wish you could see it all....

She skimmed through the body of the letter, which elaborated on the aforementioned, and skipped to the last page. *Surely there is some personal word, his steadfast love, the prayers he is offering up in my behalf. . . .*

My master Alessandro de' Medici says I am making rapid progress and should be ready to deal with some minor clients before long. I have attended several gala social events where I have met some of the senior bankers and aristocratic merchants. I believe I am able to hold forth in conversation as well as any.

I—I—I! This sounds like his personal journal, not a letter to his beloved. And the "social events" no doubt include ravishing dance partners. But she read on.

Françoise, my heart aches to be thus separated from you. My life is incomplete without you. I do not mean incomplete without a woman. I mean only you can complete my life. There is no lady in all Florence as beautiful as you nor as intelligent, gentle, and devoted to her faith. No other woman can ever bring me the happiness you have brought me. I adored you from the first moment I saw you. I do not know what more I can do for you to trust me fully, to love me without reservation. But I do crave your wholehearted love. Do you think of me more in my absence—or less? The answer to that question may be your heart alerting you to your true feelings.

I hope you are enjoying the children in your care. You were always so tender toward Etienne. I went to the magnificent Duomo yesterday and prayed God's continued protection and blessings upon you.

The apprentices will have most of the month of June off. I plan to come to my uncle's villa, and we will spend as much time together as your work will allow. The necklace I gave you for the evening at the grand duke's has forty pearls—one

*for each day more that we will be apart. If you receive my let-
ter Tuesday, count one pearl off each day until we will again
be together.*

*All my love,
Stefano*

With tears of happiness running down her cheeks, Françoise
dropped to her knees beside the bed. *Thank You, Lord Jesus.
Stefano still loves me! Heal my heart that I may love him back.* She
took the little wooden box from its secret place on the armoire's
shelf. Curled on burgundy velvet lay the pearl necklace. She
gently removed it and tied a strand of red yarn between the first
and second pearl. *Only thirty-nine days until Stefano comes.*
From that moment, her daily life at the Maffeis' was filled with
the joy of anticipation.

eleven

Françoise was startled one afternoon when a servant summoned her to the salon after lessons had ended for the day. *Surely Stefano could not be here. I have counted off only ten pearls.* Nevertheless, she pressed a cold wet cloth against her face and dried and pinched her cheeks before coming downstairs to see who awaited.

"Buona sera, Signorina Chaplain." A familiar-looking gentleman, whom she could not place, stood beside Lucrezia.

"Françoise, this is Almeni, personal manservant to Cosimo, Grand Duke of Tuscany. With your permission, I will remain to hear what he has to tell you," she said, showing a maternal interest in her children's governess.

"Good afternoon to you, signore," Françoise said, remembering him now. She was alarmed that he should be here to address her for whatever reason. "Yes, Lucrezia, please stay."

"Please, let us all sit down," said Lucrezia.

Almeni sat and placed his ankle across his opposite knee in a most casual fashion. Two other servants, who had come with him, stood silently behind his chair. "Signorina, my master, the grand duke, has found you to his liking. Your beauty and talents pleased him greatly at his dinner party you attended. You will recall it was I who suggested you be included in the invitation. He has since praised me highly for my good taste in selecting you—that is, in suggesting he invite you. I'm sure your dazzling beauty played an important role in Signore Stefano's appointment at the Medici Bank."

Stunned by his words, Françoise opened her mouth, but no words came forth.

Lucrezia, however, answered in her stead. "From the account I have heard, signore, the grand duke found Stefano sufficiently talented and worthy quite on his own. Please thank your master for his gracious words. And now—" She arose to dismiss Almeni.

"But that is not all, signora," said Almeni, staying in his casual pose and turning to Françoise. "The grand duke, himself, signorina, has sent you this token of his affection." He pulled from under his cloak an ornate gold case inlaid with mother-of-pearl in the shape of a heart. He presented it to her with a flourish. "From the Grand Duke of Tuscany to the lady he finds most charming. This is a rare honor and privilege—as I am sure you realize—for a girl of your status."

Still bewildered, Françoise took the case and opened it. Inside lay a heavy gold-chain necklace with a bejeweled cross as a pendant. To her, it seemed ugly in its exaggerated opulence and inappropriate for the Christian symbol. "Please. . . thank his highness. . . ," she said with hesitation.

"Signorina cannot possibly accept such a gift, as it in no way represents the relationship between the two," said Lucrezia firmly.

"No, of course, I cannot accept such a gift," echoed Françoise. She realized Lucrezia had been quicker than she to see the duke's unworthy intentions. She closed the case and handed it back to Almeni, who set it on the small table between them.

Almeni thoughtfully rubbed his clean-shaven chin and sat up straight but remained entrenched in his chair. He turned to the two servants behind him and gave some instructions in a low voice. The men bowed, turned, and left the villa.

"I am afraid I have not made myself clear, signorina," he said, leaning toward her and lowering his voice. "This may well be an opportunity for you to become the next Duchess of Tuscany. No one ever refuses the grand duke. That would not be a wise move for—well, that would not be wise. Tomorrow at four of the clock in the afternoon, the grand duke will send a carriage for you, complete with your personal maidservants."

The two men returned carrying a very large crate. They set

it on the floor and pried it open. Inside lay several richly adorned dresses of brocaded silk and velvet, hats with feathers, shoes, and other accessories. "These are for you, signorina. My master requests that you wear the ivory-colored costume with the scarlet cape tomorrow. Please tell these servants where you wish the articles placed."

Françoise finally gathered her wits. "Please tell the grand duke that I am indeed flattered by his offer and find the gifts beautiful, but my love is for another, and I must refuse his generous offer. Please take back the clothing. I have no need of it." She stood up. Though her words were kind enough, her voice remained firm and her fists clenched.

"No one rebuffs the grand duke," said Almeni as politely as she had spoken to him, adding a smile. He motioned his men to fasten the crate and return it to the carriage. "Someone will pay for this, signorina." With that, he turned and followed the men out the door.

The two women sighed with relief and threw their arms around each other. Françoise felt a friendship beginning between them that they had not previously known. Indeed, she had not so much as confided to her the duke's indiscretion at his dinner party. Lucrezia was still in her early twenties, vivacious and level-headed, not as slender as Françoise but quite attractive.

"I am so glad you offered to stay with me," said Françoise. "I am still innocent about the ways of the world. You are quick-thinking like my mother. It is still a mystery how he found me here and why he would be interested in me."

"The duke has eyes and ears everywhere, or he may have even called first at the Marinelli villa and learned of your whereabouts. As to his interest in you, I think that would be obvious to anyone who met you. Your beauty is unmatched. You are charming, intelligent, and pure of heart," said Lucrezia. "And actually he may have chosen Stefano for the apprenticeship in Florence to remove him from Milan—that is, to place him out of the way."

"Could my refusal harm Stefano?"

"That is possible," she said. "Officially we have rule by law, but the duke, in essence, has the power of life and death over his subjects. Milan lies outside of Tuscany, but there is no one powerful enough to oppose him if he wishes to take revenge anywhere in Italy."

"Is that what he meant by 'someone will pay for this'?" Françoise was beginning to realize the extent of what she had done by her refusal. "He could harm me or even you and your family?"

"The duke is quite unpredictable. He will return to Florence soon and may forget all about your rebuff." Then, with a smile of reassurance, she added, "You did exactly the right thing."

As they were leaving the salon, Françoise exclaimed, "Oh, no, he left this ridiculous case with the necklace here on the table! I am not yet free of this royal monster."

❧

Stefano and the two other apprentices at the Medici Bank soon began work with minor clients under Alessandro's supervision. Stefano did not share in all the amusements pursued by Luigi and Diego; nevertheless, his life outside of his duties was filled with festivals, theater, and excursions to notable sites. Never before had he found his life so pleasurably enriched—nor so surrounded by worldly temptations. The senior bankers considered him a charming asset at their social evenings. Often his host would present a daughter in the hopes he would take an interest in her that would lead to marriage. Such a rising young apprentice in the company could not help but enjoy the flattery.

At the Blue Goose Tavern, the young men sat at a table and discussed the events of the day. "Old Alessandro doesn't hang around as much as he did when we first started talking to clients," said Stefano. "I think he trusts us to know what we are doing. I'm feeling more confident."

"He checks the books every night, though," said Diego

with a sneer. "They don't pay us enough for the skills we have developed."

"It's not all that hard to make the ledgers add up and pay yourself a little extra, too," said Luigi. "That is, if anyone were so inclined. Would you be so inclined, Stefano?"

Stefano often found himself in a quandary such as this. He valued the acceptance of his peers, but at the same time he wished to follow the moral and religious standards his parents had taught him. "You are right, Luigi. Small sums could be siphoned off, I suppose," he said, measuring his words. "But I am not inclined to jeopardize my future of becoming a wealthy and prestigious banker at the wealthiest and most prestigious bank in all Europe for a few extra coins. Old Alessandro may be more alert than we give him credit for."

"You could be right, my friend," said Diego and winked at Luigi. They both laughed, and Luigi called the waitress to their table.

❧

Françoise heard the bell ringing at the front gate of the Maffei household and the voice of a man. "A letter for Signorina Françoise Chaplain," he announced to the maid who had answered the bell.

Françoise peered out the window and noticed the emblem of Tuscany on the ducal carriage, which stood near the gate. "Perhaps you would like to present the message personally to the signorina," she overheard the maid saying. "Please come in, and I will summon her." Françoise knew gossip had spread among the servants about the last time a royal messenger had called upon her. Thus the maid was no doubt excited to be privy to this ongoing drama. She hurried inside, apparently to tell Lucrezia, who in turn came to inform Françoise.

The children had just gone to the kitchen for their afternoon refreshment, which left Françoise free for a few minutes. When she entered the salon, the messenger bowed low. "Buona sera, signorina. I am Filippo, the personal manservant of Cosimo, Grand Duke of Tuscany, and I come to deliver this letter from his highness."

"Good afternoon, signore," she said and took the large folded parchment offered her. The red wax seal, which bore the imprint of the royal emblem, alarmed her, but she covered her emotion by saying, "Excuse me, signore, for asking, but I thought Almeni was the grand duke's personal servant."

Filippo appeared suddenly nervous and at a loss for words. "I can only say, signorina, that—well, he is no longer in that position. It is I who officially speaks—who represents the grand duke. Long may he live!"

"Long may he live!" she repeated. "Must I respond now to whatever this message contains, or may I read it in private?"

"You may read it in private. I come from the Uffizi Palace in Florence where the grand duke is presently in residence. He plans to vacation again in Milan in a week or so—early June. At that time he will send me here for your response. I suggest you have a letter prepared as he will want to hear your answer immediately after I request it. Good day, signorina."

❧

In near panic, Françoise hurried to look for Lucrezia. She found her chatting and laughing with her children in an alcove off the kitchen.

"Lucrezia, look what the duke sent me," she blurted out. "I cannot read such a thing alone."

"I can read it," volunteered Maria.

"So can I," said her brother.

"No, my children, this is a story only for grown-ups," their mother said with a laugh. "You may read the rabbit story to me in a little while."

"Yes, Mother," they said in unison and ran to their study room to look for the manuscript.

"Now, sit down, Françoise," Lucrezia said, "and we will discover together what his highness has devised this time."

Françoise broke the seal, breathed in deeply, then looked down at the elaborate script. "Do you suppose this is written by his own hand?"

"I doubt that. I am sure he dictated it to a scribe. Why don't you read it aloud?"

Françoise read:

My dear, precious Françoise,

I think of you night and day and am tormented by the fear that I may have offended you. Please accept my humble apology. I desire only your happiness. Since your love, at this time, belongs to another, I withdraw my proposal of marriage out of respect for you.

"That does not sound as if he is plotting revenge, would you not say?" said Lucrezia.

"But there is much more," said Françoise, noticing the second large page. She continued:

I recall the lovely music you played on the harpsichord that evening we spent together. More than a beautiful woman, you are both talented and unique among those females I have met. I am astounded that a lady could compose and play so well. Therefore, to demonstrate to you the sincerity of my apology, I have arranged a special tutor for you. He will instruct you, not only in more advanced techniques on the harpsichord, but also in music notation and composition.

I will send a carriage for you each Saturday evening so that you may meet with your instructor in the music room of my country villa there in Milan. If you wish, I will have a harpsichord delivered to the Maffei residence so that you may practice during the week. As I personally will be your patron, I can assure you that fame and fortune await you. This, my dear, is an opportunity I have never before offered to a woman.

I am very pleased you kept the jeweled necklace. Perhaps as you wear it around your neck, you will think of this unworthy man who loves only you with all his heart—but who has abandoned the pursuit of your love in return. I seek only to fulfill your desires and ambition and pray you will accept both my apology and my generous offer.

With a sincere heart, I remain your loving servant,

Cosimo,
Grand Duke of Tuscany

"My emotions are mixed, Lucrezia," Françoise said as she folded the letter and laid it on the small table between them. She expressed her thoughts aloud and weighed the situation. "I am repulsed by much of his language, and I haven't forgiven him for the way he treated me while dancing at his dinner party, but I believe both his apology and offer are sincere, don't you? He rarely comes to Milan. I don't see an evil intent here. Aside from being with Stefano, nothing could give me more pleasure than an opportunity to play the harpsichord and learn more properly how to compose music. I do want that—very much."

"His patronage would certainly provide possibilities for acceptance in the masculine music world," Lucrezia said. "Did Almeni actually offer a proposal from the duke?" she abruptly asked.

"I'm not sure." Françoise tried to remember Almeni's exact words. "I think it was more of a hint that I might become the next Duchess of Tuscany. It all happened so fast, and I was startled by it and confused. . . ."

"You didn't *accept* the necklace, as he states."

"No, I only saw it still lying on the table—after Almeni left. Of course, he had to account for it. Almeni must have told his master I accepted it, to cover forgetting it. I can't blame the duke for believing him. His offer sounds innocent enough to me. The duke spends most of his time in Florence anyway. I probably would never see him."

"Perhaps you are right. With the duke, it could be hazardous either way, though."

The children rushed up to their mother. "I found the rabbit story," said Luca, pulling it from Maria's hands.

"It was under his bed," Maria said. "He didn't put it back in the study room."

Lucrezia took the manuscript, which was a simple story her husband, Ferdinando, had written for them. "Let's think more on this, Françoise." Then turning to the children, she said, "I believe it is Luca's turn to read first."

Françoise rushed to her room, where she read the letter twice more. Then she opened her armoire and took out the little wooden box on the shelf. She sat on her bed to open it. She gently untied the red yarn and slipped it down one more pearl. *Six pearls left. He should be here before the duke demands a reply. I will ask Stefano for his advice. Oh, Stefano, I miss you so!*

twelve

Françoise released the last pearl of her necklace and laid the bit of yarn beside the box. *Stefano should arrive today!* She bathed, then donned a simple pale yellow dress, full-skirted with open neck and long, puffed sleeves. Her dark eyes and upbraided hair made a striking contrast to the pale dress. Should she or shouldn't she? The pearls lay coiled in the open box. Finally, she picked them up and clasped the strand around her neck. Looking in the oval mirror above her dressing table, she concluded, *Yes. They are for special occasions, and what could be more special than today? Stefano will know how I treasured his gift and that I counted the days upon it.*

Late in the afternoon, Maria and Luca were playing an ancient Roman game in the enclosed garden. They took turns in which one child would toss a stone into each of a series of squares drawn on the flagstones, hop through the squares, and return to the beginning without missing. Françoise sat on a garden bench. As she watched them, she thought how she had grown to love these children as her own. They were both quick of mind and body and overflowed with energy. She remembered that at the beginning she had doubted her own ability to teach. But her dear father had instilled in her and Etienne a love for learning. By emulating his methods, she had found success with her charges.

As the children played, their long shadows bounced beside them, and their cheerful voices filled the air. The sun filtered between the tall cedars and across the flowering shrubs and flagstone path. It was a mild day, full of sweet outdoor smells and the chirp of nesting birds. For Françoise, the joy of anticipation had increased as the day wore on, but now the tension of waiting turned to anxiety. *What if he doesn't come? What if he is sick or injured? Or perhaps Florence holds more excitement, and he has decided. . .*

"Françoise."

Her heart leapt to her throat at the sound of the familiar voice. Joyful tears stung the corners of her eyes and melted her doubt. She turned. There was Stefano, emerging from the doorway. His finely tailored clothing, embellished doublet, and black velvet cap announced a man of distinction. And his short beard and mustache, she noticed, were fuller now, more mature.

She stood, and he walked toward her. They reached out and clasped each other's hands and smiled with mutual elation. The children's voices hushed with shyness around a stranger.

"Time to come in Maria, Luca," Lucrezia called from the doorway, leaving the two alone in the garden.

Before either spoke, Stefano encircled her in his arms. She closed her eyes and felt his warm lips press against hers. "Oh, Stefano, I am so happy you are here."

"We belong together like this, my love," he whispered in her ear.

Françoise reeled with delight as they sat close to each other on the garden bench, her hand clasped in his. "I see you are wearing the forty-pearl necklace. But its beauty pales beside your own."

"I counted the days by tying a bit of red yarn between the pearls and moving it down once each day. You came just as you said you would on the fortieth day—today."

"And I placed little stones on my windowsill and pitched one out the window each day. I hoped you were not doing the same with your pearls."

Françoise laughed as she imagined Stefano throwing out the little rocks. "Did you by any chance pelt a passerby?"

"I never bothered to look," he said, chuckling with her. He then became more serious. "We have much to talk about. Lucrezia graciously invited me to stay here for dinner tonight.

Her husband is scheduled to arrive from Genoa at any time, and she wants me to meet him."

"They have both been so kind and generous to me," said Françoise. "Lucrezia treats me as though I were her younger sister. And I love working with little Luca and Maria. They are such dears." She laid her head on his shoulder.

"I am pleased you are happy here." He gently touched her cheek and smoothed back the wisps of hair from her face. "I want to know the family so I can more easily envision your daily life with them."

"And I want to hear more about your exciting life in Florence," she said, lifting her head and looking into his eyes. She hoped her words masked the concerns she felt. "Your letter made life there sound like a perfect paradise."

"Excitement does not always equal good, however. I need you beside me to make it a paradise."

Françoise smiled, content with his reassurance, and kissed his cheek.

Stefano responded with a lingering kiss on her mouth. "I love you, Françoise, with my whole being."

"I am so happy when I am with you," she said.

They sat quietly for a few minutes, their arms entwined about each other. Françoise knew he wanted to hear words of love from her, but the old fears gripped her heart. His mere mention of love seemed to bring forth the opposite of its intended effect. *Maybe before he leaves I can say the words he wants to hear.* But her heart again remained silent.

"I will be staying at my uncle's villa," he said. "I purchased a horse and rode it here, but I have no carriage. Tomorrow is Sunday, and I assume you are free to spend the day at the Marinelli villa. I am sure Uncle Matteo will be glad to have the family carriage brought by for you. We can all attend church service together. And afterward, you and I may stroll in the villa gardens. They should be bursting with June flowers."

"That sounds like a wonderful plan, Stefano. My Sundays

are always free days, and when Etienne is home, Signore Matteo sends a carriage for me. My brother should be there tomorrow, but I will spend the afternoon with you."

❧

The couple enjoyed the evening meal with Lucrezia, Ferdinando, and their children. Lucrezia showed approval of Stefano by the way she listened intently to his every word. After the children were dismissed from the table, Ferdinando dominated Stefano's attention by talking in detail about the fabric trade.

Lucrezia whispered to Françoise, "Have you asked his advice about Cosimo's offer?"

"Not as yet. But I will," she whispered back. The more she thought about the opportunity for her, the more she leaned toward accepting Cosimo's offer. Just as the renaissance in art had exploded into new and exciting innovations, music was beginning to find new forms as well. Lucrezia had even told her there were a few—though very few—accepted women artists. Why not female composers of music as well?

The four retired to the salon, where Lucrezia lit two whale-oil lamps. Ferdinando finally dropped his monologue about the fabric business and asked Stefano about his experiences in Florence. "Cosimo is back in residence in Florence, and rumors are flying about him," said Stefano.

"Yes, did you hear what happened to poor Almeni?" Ferdinando said, shaking his head.

"I heard. We rarely see the grand duke at the bank, but everyone follows the daily gossip about him. I guess it is true he will never remarry. He is still devoted to his wife Eleonora, all these years after her death."

Françoise was startled at the mention of something happening to Almeni and exchanged questioning glances with Lucrezia. The subject of Cosimo made her feel uncomfortable, but she wanted to know about Almeni.

But Stefano moved on. "Have you ever visited the fabulous Boboli pleasure gardens behind the Pitti Palace? I understand

Cosimo had them built for Eleonora. Cypress and hedge-lined alleys—"

"Unusual statuary, fountains, and grottoes. . ."

The men were off in the gardens and not likely to return to the subject of Cosimo himself. Françoise sighed with relief, then turned to Lucrezia to talk about the children.

ও

The Maffeis retired early and left the young couple unchaperoned in the salon. Stefano appeared not at all fatigued from his daylong ride, and Françoise felt aglow with pleasure in being near him. They sat in separate renaissance chairs but close enough for him to place his hand over hers.

"Ferdinando and Lucrezia are interesting people," he said. "I learned much about the fabric trade that will be helpful in my career. I'm afraid we failed to include you in our business conversation. But now, Françoise, I yearn to hear you talk of your concerns."

"I do have a concern I want to talk about." She smoothed her skirts and cleared her throat. It was time to present the Cosimo offer, and she must choose her words carefully. Surely he would understand that the opportunity for a musical career was as important to her as his banking career.

"Yes? You have my complete attention." He leaned toward her and took her hand again in his.

"I am pleased, Stefano, that this wonderful opportunity has come to you—to rise in the field of banking, which will be both prestigious and lucrative. It is a career to which you are well suited, and it uses your God-given talents."

"Yes. I believe God can place opportunities in our paths. He sometimes uses people—as in my case the cunning grand duke Cosimo—to open the way. Sometimes I feel unworthy at my good fortune. But go on—"

Though startled by the word *cunning*, she let it slip past without comment. "Well, Stefano, I feel that my God-given talent is to compose music."

"Yes, I would agree. And your voice is angelic. It gives me

much pleasure to hear you play and sing your psalms."

"What would you think, Stefano"—she withdrew her hand, stood, took several steps forward and back, then whirled and stood in front of him—"what if God gave me the opportunity to take lessons on the harpsichord? What if I had a powerful patron who would provide an instructor to teach me notation? What if his favor assured my success?"

"I'm astounded at these words, Françoise," he said, standing to face her on equal footing. "This is fantasy! Composition of music is not a woman's career." Rather than angry, he appeared simply shocked.

"Perhaps I will be the first," she said.

"Françoise, my darling, I want only your happiness." He took her hands and kissed her on the forehead. "What you are talking about is entering the business world—the *business* of music. There is wickedness in the business world. It is not a place for a woman, especially a pious one like you."

His voice softened, perhaps because he realized her earnestness. "Yes, if you have a chance to take advanced lessons and learn to compose, do that. But for your own pleasure and for mine."

"I have an opportunity for more than that." She sat down and looked off into her future. "Why should I not be Italy's first woman composer? There are some renowned women painters—"

"Françoise, who has offered to be your patron?"

"The same who offered opportunity to you—Cosimo, Grand Duke of Tuscany!" She had saved this information until now, as her last point of persuasion, assuming it would have the greatest impact.

Stefano slumped down in his chair and leaned forward with his head in his hands.

Stunned by his reaction, she sat down and tried to reason with him. "But if his patronage is good for you, why then is it not also good for me?"

"Because. Because you are a woman—a beautiful, desirable

woman at that. Don't you see, Françoise? It is not your career he has in mind. I saw the way he danced with you at his party—"

"I saw the way you danced with that woman," she said defensively.

"That's different. I am a man. Besides, that was not my idea, and I held her at a distance."

"And you go to social events all the time in Florence. There are bound to be beautiful young women there!"

"You have no cause for jealousy."

"Nor do you! I have absolutely no romantic interest in Cosimo. He repulses me."

"Françoise, this is not about jealousy. Trust me."

The word *trust* fell between them with an inaudible thud. Lack of trust was the one element that had built a wall between them. They both knew it. *If I am to truly love Stefano, I must trust him with all my heart. His opinion might be wrong, but I must believe his intention is pure.* The fear of betrayal welled up in her throat. She could hear Guillaume's kind and sensitive words just before his betrayal—the betrayal that caused the raging fire that burned up her already murdered father and consumed her little brother and sisters. *Perhaps Stefano's reasons are selfish, too. . . . How can I know?*

Without a word, Stefano stood, walked to the mantel, and picked up a candle in its holder. He lit it from one of the lamps, then blew out the flame in both lamps. "Come, Françoise. Walk with me to the side door. I must not arrive too late at my uncle's villa. My mother will be waiting for me."

He reached for her hand and pulled her up beside him. They walked to the door side by side, not touching. There he set the candle on a stand by the door and faced her. Françoise could see the candle flame reflected in his eyes. *He is angry with me now. I never should have brought up the subject. I could have taken the lessons without his knowledge. I may have lost him forever,* she thought. Although his face did not reveal wrath, she could not guess what emotion lay there.

"Françoise, I am pleased you told me about Cosimo's offer and your ambition to be a composer of music. You trusted me with that information."

There is that word trust *again.*

"I was quite surprised at the extent of your ambition." He placed his hands on her shoulders. She turned her face up, close to his.

"I'm sorry we argued," she whispered. "I didn't know you felt so strongly—about Cosimo."

"I managed it badly," he said, putting his arms around her and lightly kissing her forehead. "I want you to share your concerns and ambitions with me. I will always love you. No argument, large or small, will change that."

If only I could trust those words. How can I know? Perhaps it is my ambition alone that disconcerts him. Guillaume spoke such words when he meant otherwise.

"There are reasons I feel strongly about Cosimo. Especially about his offer to you. I will tell you why tomorrow when we have more time. Uncle Matteo's carriage will come for you early in the morning. We will have all day together."

He placed his lips on hers and kissed her gently but not passionately. "Good night, my love." He handed her the candlestick, and she watched him fade into the darkness of the night.

thirteen

In her room, Françoise found sleep elusive. So many confusing thoughts swirled in her head as she tossed about. Even as a child, she had harbored a dream of composing music that others would enjoy and play in the grand cities of Europe. Shortly after taking only a few lessons from her father, she had fingered the keys for her own songs. Never had she mentioned this secret desire to anyone, nor had she allowed the notion to surface in her own mind. Of course, the idea was impossible—like flying or becoming queen of France.

Cosimo had awakened that dream and offered the nearly assured possibility—and asked nothing in return. *"It is not your career he has in mind."* She remembered Stefano's words. *Cosimo withdrew his proposal and only wished me to accept his apology. What reasons will Stefano give me for refusing his offer? Stefano seems so good and pure of heart. I do so want to trust him and believe he is thinking only of my happiness. I want to love him with all my heart.*

She thought of her mother and Etienne. It would be so good to see them—and Stefano's mother and the Marinellis—as it had been three weeks since she'd spent a Sunday with them. *Mother is wise, but I know she would be against a music career for me. She is usually reluctant to accept modern ways. I didn't want Stefano to leave tonight. . . .* She finally drifted off to sleep—the memory of Stefano's uncertain kiss lingering on her lips.

❧

At the Marinelli villa, Françoise's mother asked if she and Stefano would like to worship in the family chapel. Signora Caterina had offered it to her as a place for daily prayers. It held a large Bible on a stand, and her mother came here alone

101

early every morning to read the Scriptures and to pray. "We will have no priest, but the Huguenots often met in homes without a pastor where they read the Scriptures, sang, and prayed. I usually accompany Signoras Caterina and Isabella for services at the Duomo, but Signore Matteo is home and can go with them, so if you would like. . ."

"That would please me very much, signora," said Stefano. "And you, Françoise, would that please you?" They were leaving the table after breaking their fast. The reunion had been a joyous one. Signora Isabella listened with sparkling eyes as Stefano told of his progress at the bank. Signore Matteo talked of how the new waterwheel proved more efficient than the old methods at his silk factory. He praised Etienne for his fine bookkeeping skills. Even Signora Caterina appeared happy to welcome Françoise as her guest.

"Yes, Mamma, I would like to worship in the little chapel. I miss our ways. You do not mind, Signora Caterina and Signore Matteo?"

"Not at all. We will visit with you later in the day," said Signore Matteo. "Until later." He took his wife's arm, and they went on their way.

॰॰

Stefano made the sign of the cross as he faced the altar in the little chapel. The last time he had been here was for his father's memorial service. Memories of that time and thoughts of his father and lost brother, Giulio, filled his mind. With sadness of heart, he knelt with the Chaplain family and folded his hands.

He had not thought of Giulio in some time, though he had long ago forgiven his brother for the loose words that put their family in danger and brought death to their father. If Giulio had not revealed their harboring of refugees, someone else eventually would have done so. No, he cared about his brother and prayed that wherever he might be, God would keep him safe.

And, Lord God, he prayed, moving his lips silently, *I confess my sin of straying from Your presence. I ask Your forgiveness. And*

I pray Thee for the right words to let Françoise know she should refuse Cosimo. May she and I be of one accord at the end of this day. For I love her so much. . . .

Signora Elise read aloud the sixth chapter of Matthew. These words remained in Stefano's mind, and he pondered them. "Lay not up for yourselves treasures upon earth. . . . For where your treasure is, there will your heart be also."

Françoise played the harpsichord and sang Psalm 121 as a solo. Then she asked her mother, brother, and Stefano to sing it with her a second and third time. Stefano sang along awkwardly. He noticed that Françoise's face was radiant with the joy of music and the spiritual inspiration of the words: "I will lift up mine eyes unto the hills, from whence cometh my help. My help cometh from the Lord. . . ."

Of course, she wants to pursue this wonderful gift God has given her, he thought. Yet he had nothing to suggest to her because he knew Cosimo's plan to be a fraud.

Stefano had given plans for this day much thought. With his uncle's permission, he had arranged for Sergio, the stable hand, to accompany him and Françoise to the Adda River for a picnic. The plan included Etienne. He and Sergio, who was in his late teens, would fish the river. They would all go on horseback, and if they were successful, fish would be the evening meal for all back at the villa. His aunt Caterina even set out a riding hat and boots for Françoise, as she had hardly come prepared for such a venture.

Françoise accepted his idea. "It will be so refreshing to be out in the countryside."

At his aunt Caterina's suggestion, Françoise packed a basket, and Stefano tied it behind his saddle. The four rode down cobbled streets that soon turned to packed earth and finally trampled grass as the town disappeared behind them. The morning was pleasantly warm with sunshine and blue skies. They rode across green meadows, past grape vineyards on hillsides and groves of olive trees. They could see a hazy outline of snowcapped Alps in the far distance to the north.

Stefano and Françoise rode side by side, followed by Etienne and Sergio.

"Do you see that row of trees up ahead?" said Stefano, pointing. "The river lies just beyond. Are you comfortable enough with your steed to canter?"

Françoise hesitated. "I'm on sidesaddle." Stefano caught the twinkle in her eye. "But I'm ready. Let's go."

Etienne and Sergio took off at full gallop, but Stefano kept his horse to a slower pace next to Françoise. Soon they all dismounted at the river's edge.

"That was good sport," said Etienne. "I haven't ridden since we lived in La Rochelle." He tied his horse to a sapling, as did the others. Stefano noticed that the boy's face shone with pleasure and good health.

"Nor have I," said Françoise, giving her brother a hug around the shoulders. "The fresh air is good for all of us. I miss you and Mamma, Etienne. Do you get outside much?"

"Somewhat. I gather mulberry leaves for the silkworms in the mornings," he said. "Then I work with the ledgers in the afternoon. Or sometimes I do bookkeeping all day. I like that work, but it's tedious."

Françoise untied a rolled-up blanket from behind her saddle. Etienne helped Sergio check the fishing nets and untangle them.

"It's a hard life, is it not, working in the factories?" asked Stefano, unfastening the picnic basket.

Etienne shrugged his shoulders. "Not as bad as some. Signore Matteo makes sure we have enough to eat and insists we keep the barracks clean. I hear awful stories about how some boys are treated, especially the wool dyers." He bit a knot in the net with his teeth to loosen it. "I'm lucky to be where I am."

"Someday I hope to get you apprenticed at the bank with me."

"I would like that," he said and grinned. "Then maybe I could sleep where there aren't so many fleas. They are a terrible pest this year."

"You don't still have those horrible rats, I hope." Françoise shuddered, then spread the blanket on the grass.

Etienne laughed. "We find dead ones now. There was one on my mat the other morning, all puffy with blood oozing out its nose." He puffed out his cheeks and made a face.

"Oh, Etienne, stop that!" She cringed.

"We'd best start throwing our nets if we're going to catch anything. It's already late," said Sergio as he rolled up the nets. "There's a good spot in the cove just past the bend in the river." He and Etienne took a loaf of bread and headed out through the brush on foot.

Stefano set the basket in the middle of the spread-out blanket and lifted the napkin covering the food. "I'm hungry. Are you likewise?"

Françoise sat down on the other side of the basket. "Yes, but I didn't pack much. Caterina generously told me to take anything I wished from the kitchen, but I wasn't sure. She is so reserved in her attitude toward me that I never know what she is thinking." She set a loaf of bread, two different cheeses, and a bowl of blueberries on the large linen napkin.

Stefano took out a flask of water and set it beside the food. "You remind my aunt of her daughter in Rome. They haven't seen her or their grandchildren in several years. But I know another woman whose feelings are difficult to discern. . . ."

He looked earnestly into her eyes.

"Some woman in Florence, you must mean." She bit her lip as if to stifle a wry grin.

Stefano read the gesture as flirtatious. "As to the women in Florence"—he dismissed them with a flourish of his hand—"I have no desire to know their thoughts and feelings." But he was overcome with a desire to know this woman's feelings toward him. Françoise sat demurely across from him, her skirt spread out about her, and the velvet riding hat cocked to one side. So beautiful. The river burbled behind her, and wild red poppies dotted the grass around them. *Will you ever love me with your whole heart, Françoise. Why can you not trust me?*

Stefano longed to hold her in his arms, for her to be his wife. Though in Florence he imagined himself successful and self-confident, he now felt weak and vulnerable as he looked into her eyes. *No, I do not know what she is thinking. Nor do I have words to reach her.*

"Should we not ask God's blessings on this food, Stefano?"

Her logical question offered an escape from the intensity of his fervor. "Yes. Yes, of course." Stefano pulled up to a kneeling position.

"Heavenly Father," he prayed. "We thank Thee for the blessings You have bestowed upon us and Your protection in times of trouble. Bless this food we are about to consume. And I ask that You bring Françoise and me to mutual understanding. In the name of the Father and of the Son and of the Holy Spirit, amen."

"Amen," said Françoise without commenting on the "mutual understanding" part of his prayer. She broke the loaf and handed Stefano half. "Do you suppose Sergio and Etienne will catch any fish?"

"It is late in the day, and the sun is out, but they may be lucky." He spread cheese on a morsel of bread, took a bite, and chewed it slowly. *Perhaps I should confess some of my thoughts and shortcomings if I truly wish for mutual understanding.*

"Françoise, the Scripture your mother read this morning struck me. You know, about your heart being where your treasure is."

"Yes, Stefano, I believe that. My treasure is my faith in the Lord God. I believe He is always with me. He comforts me when I am overcome with sorrow." She pulled a stem from a blueberry and popped the fruit in her mouth.

"You have no doubts about God then, do you, Françoise? Even after all the deaths in your family?"

She wiped her fingertips on the corner of the napkin and looked at him more seriously. "I still grieve and cry sometimes. And I miss my loved ones terribly. But I don't think God is to blame. The evil in the world is to blame. There will always be evil, but, no, I have never doubted God's goodness. Have you?"

"I am not the good person you always say I am, Françoise. Most of my life has been spent on the farm you saw. It was a simple life, and out in the fields it was easy to feel God's presence. My mother and father were both strong believers like you. I knew nothing else." He took a drink of water from the flask while searching for his next words. "In the exciting city of Florence, I found it easy to forget about my upbringing. My love for you has never wavered, but I confess to you I did not pray for you every day as I had promised."

He thought he could see hurt in her eyes, but he continued.

"I spend much of my time with decadent fellows who I know are stealing from the bank. I relish my successes, and I have enjoyed the flattery of famous men who have introduced their daughters to me. Temptations surround me every day, and I fear I will give in to them. I haven't exactly doubted God's goodness, but I think I blame Him for my father's death. After all, he was serving Him. That is hard to accept, so I avoid prayer and attending services."

Françoise took his hand. "I think I know how you feel. It's just that, in my case, God is my refuge and strength. I run to Him because that is where I find comfort. It is not a struggle for me."

"That is because you have never drifted far from Him. When I heard of my father's death, I was already caught up in wearing handsome clothes and enjoying great art and was eager to impress important people. Nothing is wrong with these things, but that was where I thought my treasure lay. When I am here with you, I know I must return to my faith, for that is my true treasure. And next to that is you, Françoise."

His heart leapt with joy when Françoise looked up at him and smiled. That, he knew, meant she accepted him—wavering faith and all.

fourteen

After eating and repacking the basket, Stefano strolled along the riverbank holding Françoise's hand. They stopped to let a wild goose with several goslings cross their path to the water's edge. Stefano had kept a chunk of bread, and together they pitched crumbs to the birds, who quickly devoured them.

"We shouldn't leave the horses unguarded," said Stefano. "Even though I can still see them from here, I would hate for bandits to take them."

They turned and retraced their steps.

"Stefano, you were going to tell me why you feel so strongly about Cosimo and why I should not allow him to provide lessons for me."

Stefano had put off the subject for fear of alienating Françoise or that she might not believe him. But she seemed receptive now. He felt a closeness between them—and hadn't she brought up the subject?

He cleared his throat and chose his words carefully. "I am not part of the high society of Florence, but I am often in contact with those who frequent the Uffizi Palace. A favorite topic of gossip among them is the Medici family and especially Cosimo, the grand duke."

"But surely you know how rumors spread. Often there is no thread of truth in them," objected Françoise.

"Yes, of course," began Stefano, concerned that his words might lead again to argument. "Cosimo makes love to many women from all walks of life."

"I thought you said Cosimo remained devoted to his dead wife after all these years."

"That is true. But in his prolonged grief, he has sought distraction by indulging in a thousand follies. Few women turn him away as he showers them with gifts of beautiful gowns and jewelry."

Stefano noticed a troubled expression pass across Françoise's face. *Surely Cosimo has not already sent her such gifts.* "The harpsichord lessons would be taken at his country villa, would they not?"

"Yes, once a week. That was what he offered," she said weakly. "But he said he would send a harpsichord to the Maffei house so that I could practice. He isn't in Milan that often."

They were back near the horses and sat down on a large shelf of rock overlooking the river. "Françoise, my dear," he said gently. "If he is there once a week or every six months—it doesn't matter. With his wealth, the price of a harpsichord and lessons is nothing. Forgive me if this offends you, but I believe he is preparing to take you as one of his mistresses."

Françoise gasped, then blurted out, "He asked me to *marry* him!"

Stefano felt the blood drain from his face. "And you said. . ."

Françoise slumped, her head in her hands.

If she said yes, that is not good. If she said no, that is dangerous. Both our lives could be in jeopardy. "Françoise, it is of utmost importance that you tell me everything. Your life could be in danger." He took her hand.

"Oh, Stefano." She gripped his hand and looked up at him. "I am trapped by my own ignorance. Lucrezia warned me that might be so—but she said I did the right thing." Tears stung her eyes. "I have been so foolish."

"Please, Françoise, you must tell me everything."

"I haven't given him an answer about the lessons."

"When did you first see him after we attended his dinner party?"

"I haven't seen him, Stefano." She took a lace handkerchief from her sleeve and wiped her nose. "Almeni came to the Maffei house one day."

"Almeni!"

"I can't tell you. I am too ashamed." She stared out over the river and sighed. "What happened to Almeni? You and Ferdinando referred to him at dinner last evening."

"I didn't want to tell you this, but if Almeni is involved, every detail becomes more important. If I ask you to trust me with the complete scenario, I must tell you all I know, also—and I will."

"So what happened to Cosimo's personal servant?"

"There are many rumors about Cosimo stating adamantly that he would never remarry. Yet he would send Almeni forth to look for young, beautiful, and vulnerable women for an evening of pleasure. If Cosimo is attracted to a specific lady, Almeni must not return empty-handed. Almeni has been known to issue hints of marriage to convince the woman in question. Is that what happened to you?"

"I will tell you, Stefano, but it embarrasses me to talk about it. Please finish about Almeni first."

"Cosimo has a mistress who lives with him at the Uffizi. Her name is Eleonora, the same as his deceased wife. Eleonora degli Albizzi, a beautiful leading lady in Florence. She has been with him for some time and has even borne him a son. Some believed he might marry her in spite of his oft-declared intention to the contrary.

"Almeni—known for talking when he should not—warned Cosimo's son that his father intended to marry Eleonora. His son had always been against the idea as he felt remarriage would dishonor his mother. Enraged, he confronted his father. Then Cosimo, furious that Almeni had spread a false rumor, turned on his servant. Supposedly he yelled, 'Almeni, get out of my sight! Get out now! And never count on me for anything whatsoever again!'

"Almeni assumed the duke would soon get over his anger and forgive him, as such outbursts had occurred before. He stayed elsewhere in Florence for a few days, then returned to his quarters in the Pitti Palace. Cosimo happened to be in the Pitti that day and, upon seeing him, shouted, 'Traitor! Traitor!'

He lost all control of himself and drove a hunting spear completely through his body. They say he has no remorse, and because he is the grand duke, the Signorie will not even attempt to bring the murderer to justice."

"That is both shocking and frightening!" Françoise straightened and looked boldly at Stefano. "I never liked Almeni, but he certainly did not deserve such a fate."

"When did he first come to the house?"

"Let me think. I believe it was very shortly after I received your letter."

"That would be about five weeks ago, near the end of April, would it not?"

"Yes, that sounds about right. When was Almeni killed?"

"Probably the middle of May," Stefano said.

"I confess, Stefano, that I was one of those women Cosimo sent gowns and jewelry to. I refused them. Rather, Lucrezia did. She was with me. But when we told the servants to take away the crates of clothing, they forgot to take a necklace he had sent. When he left, Almeni said, 'Someone will pay for this.' "

"And that is the last you have heard from him?"

"Yes, from Almeni. But another servant delivered a letter to me from Cosimo just over a week ago. I think his name was Filippo, and he seemed nervous when I asked about Almeni. I will show you the letter. The strange thing is that, in the letter, Cosimo apologized for offending me and said he was withdrawing his proposal for marriage. Oddly, he never really proposed to me. Almeni merely hinted that I might become the next duchess. And Cosimo wrote he was pleased I had accepted the necklace. I did not accept it. Almeni forgot to take it."

"It appears that Almeni falsified his report to his master. Cosimo may even have authorized him to offer a proposal in case you refused to come to him." Stefano scratched his head. "I find it difficult to believe Cosimo would be so generous as to launch your musical career after you rebuffed him. That is not his nature. Unless the offer is a way ultimately to humiliate you. That could be his way of taking revenge. He could get your hopes up, seduce you, then let you fall."

"He *has* humiliated me. I have something else to tell you, Stefano. The night of his dinner party when we were dancing, he kissed me against my will. I didn't want to tell you then as your future depended on his favor. My own pride and ambition blinded me to his evil intentions. And now I have placed both our lives in danger."

Stefano's indignation rose anew by the duke's actions, but he spoke calmly. "No, Françoise, you have done nothing wrong. You were courageous in refusing him. But have you answered his letter about the lessons?"

"Not yet. The servant who delivered it told me Cosimo would be in Milan in early June. I was to have my written response prepared when the servant came for it. I was torn in my decision. But it is very plain to me now. I will refuse his offer of lessons."

"Good. That is a good decision."

"But our lives will be in danger."

"Perhaps. Or perhaps not. He has probably blamed all his romantic troubles on Almeni. Let us hope and pray he does not send for your answer. But you'd best have a letter written and ready. This is already the first week of June. The servant could arrive any day." He placed his hand, firm and protective, over hers, then raised her hand to his lips for a soft kiss. "Would you like my help in penning your letter?"

"Oh, yes, Stefano. You are so much wiser than I."

"No, you are the wiser. You have kept faith with your religion. By your piety, you have shown me always to seek the 'Rock that is higher than I,' as the psalmist says. The greatest danger to our lives is straying from the teachings of our Lord and Savior, Jesus Christ."

"Yet my piety kept me innocent of evil and blinded me from detecting Cosimo's intent."

"Yes." Stefano chuckled in spite of the seriousness of the

dilemma. "It just proves that two people together are better than one in facing life's challenges. Do you not agree?"

A smile tipped the corners of her mouth. Stefano took that as an affirmative to his question. *She is beginning to see we belong together, that we should become one. And she is entrusting me with this quandary—even to reading and helping her answer the letter. If only her heart would speak.*

fifteen

Etienne and Sergio returned with empty nets. "The fish were all too small to keep," announced Sergio.

"Save one," added Etienne with exuberance. "We made a little fire and roasted and ate it. We would have shared it with you two, but we thought—" Etienne blushed and looked back and forth between his sister and Stefano. "It would not have been enough for dinner tonight."

Françoise was pleased to see her brother so happy and carefree, as a youth should be. He had endured as much hardship and grief as she. She regretted he had to work long hours in the factory and take on adult responsibilities at such a young age.

The four repacked their horses and headed back to the Marinelli villa. They arrived late but in time for the evening meal, after which Stefano accompanied Françoise in the carriage to the Maffei house.

"I will return late tomorrow afternoon after you have finished tutoring the children," Stefano said as a servant arrived at the gate to escort her in. "It is most urgent that we draft the letter as soon as possible. But it would be inappropriate for me to come inside now as it is close to midnight."

"What if Cosimo demands an answer before we are ready?" Françoise furrowed her brow.

"I need to read his letter in order to—" Stefano hesitated, then stopped short, as if suddenly struck with an idea. "Write a response tonight, just in case. And the most effective argument you could make would be the claim that you are betrothed to another."

She smiled up at him. "Come anytime after three of the clock. That is when the children meet with their mother for refreshment. I am sure Lucrezia will not begrudge me the time with you. Especially considering the gravity of answering the letter."

He encircled her in his arms. Their lips met in mutual accord. "And I will write the response as you have suggested—just in case," she whispered.

≈

The next morning, Stefano availed himself of the books in his uncle's library. He came across one called *New Trade Routes from Columbus to the Present* and was deeply absorbed in it when his mother appeared at the door.

"Do come in, Mother," he said, laying aside the tome.

"I don't wish to interrupt your study," she said.

"Not at all. Come in and sit down. I want to spend some time with you. I am reading about trade routes to the New World. A bank takes a high risk in loaning to a shipping company. So many vessels are lost to storms and pirates."

"It pleases me, Stefano, to see you always seeking new knowledge. It will lead to great success, I am sure. You are a good son and bring honor to me—and your late father, as well. He would be so proud of your accomplishments. You are the only one I have left in the world," she said as she took a chair beside him.

"Whatever good there is, Mother, was instilled in me by you and my father," said Stefano. "But I am not the only one you have. Your sister Josephine in Bordeaux loves you and would take you in. And Giulio may yet be alive. Let us hope he has been spared."

"I pray for him constantly and trust he made his way to the Sorbonne in Paris. Like you, he loved to study. Yes, I do still have Josephine, but I am happier in my native Italy. Mattio and Caterina have been very good to me. They, of course, grieve the death of Pietro along with me. Josephine never cared for Pietro. And Elise is a dear woman. Her religion is very real and sincere, even if her customs are different from ours. I remember how frightened I was of her and her children when they took refuge in our barn. I feared they might have brought the seeds of the plague with them."

"Yes, now we love the Chaplains as our own family." Stefano stood and returned the book to its place on the shelf. He turned and faced her. "Mother, you know I want to marry Françoise."

"And she is willing. We all know that."

"I don't feel comfortable returning to Florence without a betrothal." He sat down and tapped his fingers on the chair arm.

"It doesn't seem prudent for you to wait for her love in return—if that is what you are asking me. Most betrothals are made, as you know, without considering the girl's wishes or sometimes even the man's. Of course, there is no urgency. You will not be financially established for at least a couple of years."

"Yet life is so uncertain," said Stefano. *What if Cosimo makes demands of Françoise or tries to carry out his revenge?* He didn't wish to burden his mother with the dilemma, but he did seek her counsel. "I want her to feel more secure, better protected, while I am separated from her."

"Remember, Son, that you are the one who decided to postpone the betrothal until she could wholeheartedly express her love to you. You must admit that is a farfetched idea, a desire for perfection that few ever know. Her love for you will come with the consummation of your vows—or at least with the joy of children. That is the natural way."

"Thank you, Mother. I will consider your words. And remember, when our home is established, you will always be an important part of it."

The two continued to converse on other topics, mostly memories of their life on their farm in France near Angoulême.

෴

Stefano arrived at the Maffei house in a light one-horse carriage borrowed from his uncle Matteo. He served as his own driver and tied the horse at the gatepost. A servant let him in and notified Françoise of her visitor. She descended the staircase with Luca and Maria following. The children were laughing until they saw Stefano.

"Buona sera, signore," the children said in unison.

"Good afternoon, children. Have you had a good lesson?"

"I spelled the most words correctly," bragged Luca.

"I missed only one," said Maria. "We both guessed at it. But Luca just guessed right by accident, signore."

"You are both good spellers, children," said Françoise, giving them each a pat on the head. "Now run along to the garden. Your mother is waiting."

"You will make a wonderful mother someday, Françoise. The children seem to adore you."

"I have always loved children," she said as they both took seats in the salon. "I did much of the rearing of my young siblings who died in the fire. I was only five when Etienne was born, but I remember caring for him as a baby. We've always been very close."

"I noticed that, seeing the two of you together yesterday by the river." Stefano thought of his mother's words about love for a husband coming with the joy of children. "Do you look forward to having your own children, Françoise?"

"Do you mean *our* children, Stefano?" She lowered her long lashes and blushed. "But right now my mind is focused on answering this letter." She handed him a folded parchment.

Stefano felt joy well up within him. *Our children?* But he took the parchment without comment. He read it silently while Françoise sat nervously fiddling with her handkerchief.

The letter's content twisted his elated emotion into anger. "The scoundrel!" Stefano threw it on the table and paced the floor, his face flushed. "I see, Françoise, how you could easily be taken in. He makes it sound as though he only wishes to serve as your humble patron, promising you fame and fortune. But it is a ruse!"

"I know, Stefano. I see now how foolish I was even to consider accepting. It is not necessary to convince me further." She sounded peeved at his revisiting the argument.

He sat down and looked directly into her eyes, his anger

faded. In a much gentler voice, he quoted from Cosimo's letter, " 'Since your love at this time belongs to another. . . .' You told Almeni that?"

"I did," said Françoise. "It's the sort of strategy you suggested yesterday." The fluttering of her eyelashes did not match the business tone of her voice. "I worked late last night trying to compose a response—just in case. But I am not a scholar like you. Here's what I have been working on." She handed him a paper with cross-outs and rewritten phrases.

Stefano chuckled as he tried to make out what she had written.

"Never mind," she said, laughing with him. "I would not accept such writing from my young pupils! Just start over and tell me what to say. I know nothing about writing to royalty." She snatched the paper from him.

"It *is* illegible," he teased. "Would you be so kind as to read it to me?"

" 'To His Highness, Cosimo'—is that how I should address him?"

"That is proper, but I would add, 'Grand Duke of Tuscany.' Read on."

" 'I wish to thank you for your most generous and thoughtful offer of providing me with harpsichord lessons. I deeply appreciate your interest in furthering my musical career with your patronage. But I must refuse.' "

She paused to lend emphasis to the next line. " 'I am betrothed to another, and he disapproves of married women taking on a professional career. I am obligated as his future wife to obey him in this regard.' "

"That is absolutely perfect, short and final. You are a scholar—and a diplomat, as well. I would not add or delete a single word."

"Do you really like it? Perhaps I should add, 'And please don't murder me.' "

"Let's not be too direct with our intent," said Stefano, laughing. "I do very much like the 'betrothed' part. We will talk more on that subject later."

"And the 'obey' part? You liked that, too, I suppose?" Françoise grinned and looked at him sideways as she took paper and quill from the writing stand that stood in the corner of the room.

Stefano loved her even more in this coquettish mood. *"Please don't murder me." How droll, indeed! But we must agree on the betrothal before this day is out,* he thought. "Yes, of course, men always like to be obeyed," he answered in a light-hearted tone.

"Should I use a blunt or pointed quill?"

"I suggest you use neither but rather allow me to be your scribe. You do want the old rogue to be able to read it, don't you?" He stood close beside her at the writing stand and examined the various quills. "This one will do."

"Very good. You write, and I will dictate my letter."

The two worked together, enjoying a task they had both dreaded. Françoise praised Stefano's penmanship—precise and steady with a bit of a flare, a style he had worked hard to master at the bank. Françoise added her carefully penned signature to her elegant words. They closed the letter with sealing wax and placed it on the shelf in the writing stand.

"I hope Cosimo will never request my response. But if he does, we are ready. I will put the ugly necklace he gave me with it."

"Good," said Stefano. "That task is finished. Let us go for a carriage ride and enjoy this lovely spring weather."

⁊⁊

Lucrezia had generously given Françoise the rest of the afternoon off, and she was delighted to accept Stefano's offer of a carriage ride—wherever it might lead. She sat beside him now as they turned onto a familiar street, the Via Padova. They passed his uncle's villa and arrived at the Piazza del Duomo, a large square next to the cathedral.

"Let's stop here and stroll a bit," suggested Stefano.

Françoise was in full agreement, and Stefano quickly

alighted and offered his hand to help her descend. They walked past the busy market on one side of the piazza and commented on the various types of merchandise. Soon they arrived at the far side, where only a few people milled about. In the shade of a large tree, they found a stone bench where they could sit and face the looming Duomo with its maze of marble spires.

"What an amazing architectural wonder!" exclaimed Stefano. "My mother used to bring me and Giulio here as young children to play in the piazza—just as those little fellows are doing." Four children, under the watchful eye of their governess, were feeding the pigeons, then rushing at them to watch them fly up.

"It is a beautiful cathedral. God's house," said Françoise, then turned to him with concern. "You still have heard no word from Giulio?"

"No. I need to make a trip back to France soon to check on the farm. I do hope Gaston and Claire have managed it well. I will not be able to collect the year's rent until after harvest. I hope someone there will have news about my brother."

"Will it not be dangerous to return?" Françoise's fear of losing him increased with the emotion that sprang unbidden from her heart.

"Danger, illness, and death loom everywhere as we both know, Françoise. I must do what I must do. But we have this moment in time to live to the fullest."

"You are right, Stefano," she said with a smile. "I am happy this moment—here—with you." And, like Stefano, she realized how fragile and temporary this moment was. For the first time, she understood that her grief—rather than closing the door to life—could open the way to living more fully.

"And I am happy—with you." He reached out and laced his fingers with hers. "Françoise, I don't want to rush you or ask any more of you than you can give. But I must go back to Florence soon. We have only two more Sundays together. Every moment I am with you is precious. I worry about

Cosimo. He could abduct you at will. He could easily discover through the church records that no betrothal is recorded. . . ." He continued to ramble, talking rapidly and defensively.

"Hush," she whispered and placed a soft fingertip to his moving lips. "I love you."

He stopped short, surprise clearly written across his face. "You—you love me? With all your heart?"

She lowered her eyelashes and squeezed his hand. "I love you, Stefano. Accept that as true and don't press for more. I am ready for our betrothal." *Please, Stefano, don't reject the part because it is not the whole. Allow me to give you my wounded heart in stages.*

With his hands, he tipped her face toward his and kissed her fervently. "I love you, Françoise."

sixteen

To return, Stefano drove the carriage down a different route. Françoise felt a sense of peace and happiness within. Stefano sat close to her, as they both talked openly of their new commitment.

"Are you content for our betrothal ceremony to take place at the door of the Duomo? We have never discussed our difference in religion," said Stefano.

"If our fathers were still living and drawing up the contract and if we were still in France, that would certainly be a problem," said Françoise. She arranged her skirts more securely around her legs, while trying to imagine what her father would think of her betrothal ceremony at a cathedral. "I still prefer the manner of worship with which I grew up. But there is no such congregation here in Milan that I know of. Mother and I, and sometimes Etienne when he is with us, are the only ones who practice it."

"Less than ten years ago, Rome declared that marriage must be performed in the church—to be legal and binding," he said, seeming to urge her toward a decision.

"I live in Italy now. We are both believers in God, so religion should only be something to bring us closer together. I will abide by your wishes and whatever is required."

"Thank you, Françoise. I was afraid this would be difficult for you."

"I believe peace is better than conflict. I've never understood religious wars. . . . Look, Stefano, what is going on up ahead?" She pointed in the direction.

He slowed the horse and carriage, and they watched the bizarre activity at a house nearby. Two men worked quickly to carry three dead bodies, one at a time, out the front door.

They placed them in a cart and threw a blanket across them. An elderly woman stood on the step wringing her hands and sobbing.

Françoise recalled the man who had died at the port in Bordeaux. She had witnessed the agony up close while Stefano and Etienne arranged for their family's passage. In fear, she clung to Stefano's arm and whispered, "The plague!"

"You may be right," said Stefano, his voice strained. "Why else would they collect the dead in this manner—without ceremony?" He turned the horse around and urged him into a trot as they headed back toward the Duomo. "On my way here from Florence, I stopped at an inn for the night. When I said I was going to Milan, the innkeeper warned me of cases in the city. I never saw any evidence until now. It often comes with the warmer weather."

They rode back in silence. She felt their love was firm, but the happiness of the afternoon was crowded out by fear. Suddenly, dark clouds moved across the blue skies and a wind whipped around them, fluttering their clothing. She had neglected to bring a cape because of the earlier warm sunshine. She shuddered from the horror of the scene as much as from the chill in the air. Stefano lashed the horse to go faster.

With rain threatening and dusk darkening, Stefano bid Françoise good night hurriedly at the door with a promise to come for her on Sunday.

ॐ

At the Marinelli villa on Sunday, Stefano and his uncle Matteo met with a notary—a rather rotund fellow with ruddy cheeks. The three sat around a table in the library. The notary cleared his throat and intoned the words he customarily used. "This begins the first of the three stages in the marriage ceremonies, called the *impalmare*. I believe you have already arranged for the betrothal ceremony at the doors of the Duomo next Sunday, where the couple will pledge their intention to marry. Much later, in a few years or so, the final wedding and consummation of the vows will follow."

The notary turned to Uncle Matteo. "I see from the figures you provided me that Signore Stefano, your nephew, is presently earning a mere thirty florins a year as an apprentice. When do you expect him to have an income sufficient to support a wife and possibly children?"

Stefano opened his mouth to respond, but his uncle answered for him.

"As I mentioned before, he and his mother have an annual income from a farm in France, but that is uncertain. His mother is secure living here with Caterina and me. She is my brother's widow."

"Then his present salary is the sole income the young couple will have to depend on?"

"Yes," said Stefano.

"No," said Uncle Matteo. "In two years, possibly three, I believe Stefano will have advanced to a junior position at the Medici Bank in Florence. Stefano has told me he wishes both of their widowed mothers to live with them as well as his young brother-in-law-to-be. By that time, Etienne will be ready for an apprenticeship at the bank and should not be a financial burden."

Though Stefano knew it was proper for the older man to do the speaking, he felt somewhat embarrassed.

The notary continued, looking only at Uncle Matteo. "And you have one more item to reveal, I believe." He tapped on the document and slid it toward the older man.

"Yes, my wife and I will provide both the betrothal and the wedding meals and all the expenses of the ceremonies." He paused and grinned broadly. "And one month before the wedding, we will provide the couple a sum equal to four hundred florins to set up their household."

Astounded, Stefano could not keep silent at this surprising offer. "Uncle Matteo, you need not—"

His uncle pointed to the figure on the document and showed it to Stefano. "It is the least I can do to honor my brother's memory. It gives me much pleasure that I am in a position to do so. Our daughter in Rome has married well and has no need of our support."

"Then I will say thank you for your most generous offer. Have you told my mother?" Though startled and hesitant to accept such a gift, he nevertheless felt it ungracious to refuse.

"Not as yet." He smiled and patted Stefano's shoulder. "I will tell her when she and Françoise's mother come in for the signing of the documents and the handfasting."

Stefano knew that would be his cue to bow out.

"When the agreement is final," the notary concluded, "the two families will line up facing each other. Each person will formally shake the hand of the members of the opposite family. This handfasting will complete the *impalmare* and seal the agreement between the families."

&

Françoise, Etienne, and their mother emerged from the private chapel where they worshiped together. Earlier Stefano had accompanied his mother to the Duomo.

"Let us retire to the smaller salon where we can visit together as a family," suggested her mother. Signoras Caterina and Isabella had chosen to stroll in the gardens until they were called to the *impalmare*.

"I shall brew us some herbal tea and be with you shortly," said Françoise, heading for the kitchen.

Soon she joined her mother and brother in the salon with a tray of cups and a kettle. "There cannot be much to negotiate," she said, setting the tray on a central table. "My dowry has, no doubt, been confiscated by the state of France. We really have nothing to offer."

"You, Daughter, are the greatest prize Stefano will receive," said her mother as she poured the three cups of tea. "And you have your *cassone* that Signora Caterina had her woodcarvers make for you. Do you still add items to it?"

"Yes, I do," said Françoise. She glowed with excitement and the happiness of love. "I brought a list with me, which I gave to Signore Matteo. Lucrezia said I must, as the items would be listed in the document of assets. I have six dresses, several nightgowns, a peignoir, undergarments, a tablecloth, napkins, and embroidered towels, and I don't remember what else, but they are all on the list."

"And lots of handkerchiefs, no doubt," said Etienne. "You always have a lace-trimmed handkerchief up your sleeve. Even on that long trip from France when you had only one dress."

"I did," said Françoise with a laugh. "Dear Signora Isabella had given me three, and I washed them out at every opportunity."

"I wish we had our own house and land again," said Etienne.

"When we are married, you will have a home—with Stefano and me and Mamma. I am sure Stefano would wish it thus."

"And probably his mother as well," added her mother. "Perhaps we will all live in Florence."

"Stefano said he would try to apprentice me at the bank when I am older. How old does a bank apprentice have to be? I'm twelve now."

"Maybe fifteen because you are smart and have already had experience with ledgers," said his mother. "That's only three years away."

"If I live that long," he said as if joking.

Françoise remembered the incident she and Stefano had seen on their outing. One of the three dead bodies being carried out was a child. *The plague has already struck Milan!* But she said nothing.

Mira, the head house servant, appeared in the doorway. "Signora and signore, the gentlemen await you in the library. And, signorina, may I bring you a fresh pot of herbal tea?"

"No, thank you, Mira. I believe I will walk in the gardens." She knew and accepted the fact that the future bride and groom were excluded from the *impalmare*. Stefano would look for her there.

Stefano, Uncle Matteo, and the notary stood when Signora Elise and Etienne entered the library. His mother and Aunt Caterina were already seated, with hands folded, at the table. Stefano introduced the new arrivals to the notary. "This is Signora Elise Chaplain, mother of the bride-to-be, and Françoise's surviving brother, Etienne. I will dismiss myself for the formal handfasting."

After they had all greeted one another, Signora Elise caught Stefano's arm and whispered, "You will find her in the gardens."

He nodded acknowledgment and quickly made his exit.

seventeen

Françoise arose the following Sunday before daybreak, excited and eager to see Stefano. They had spent only a couple of evenings together that week, and he planned to leave early on the morrow to return to Florence. Never had she felt so certain that her life should be permanently entwined with Stefano's.

With care, she bathed, washed her long dark hair, and put on a dressing gown. Just as the sun was coming up over the distant hills, she stepped out on the balcony to brush her hair and let it dry in the sunlight.

A timid knock at the door stirred her from her dreams of happiness with Stefano. "Who is it?" she called.

"I'm Maria."

When Françoise opened her door, little Maria was picking up a tray where she had set it in order to knock. "Mother said I could bring you this and I could stay a few minutes if you didn't mind."

"Of course, my little lady. Come in." She took the tray from the child's hands. "Let's go out on the balcony where it is sunny."

"Your hair is long and pretty," Maria said, following Françoise outside. "I've never seen it like that before, all wavy down your back."

Françoise set the tray of hot milk, fresh bread, jam, and cheese on a small table on the balcony. "Your mother is going to braid it up for me in a little while. You may stay and watch," she said. "But how very pretty you are in your little silk dress and blue vest."

"Thank you, signorina. I want Mother to braid my hair, too, like yours." She shook her long curls. "Will you go away when you marry Signore Stefano?"

"We won't be married for a long time, so I will still be your governess. Today we just promise to marry," she said as she sipped milk from the cup. "Would you like something to eat?"

"No, thank you, signorina. Mother said to say I have already eaten."

"And have you?"

"Yes," she said with a giggle.

Maria is such a precious child. I lost so many people I loved, Françoise thought, *but now my heart overflows with love for new ones God has brought into my life. Not just Stefano, but the children and all the kind people who make up my life. And I still have Mamma and Etienne. How I love them, too!*

☙

Stefano was no less excited than Françoise as he dressed for their betrothal ceremony. His uncle Matteo had sent him a servant to lace his black embossed doublet and help with the fine details of his dressing. He wore full, gartered breeches, soft leather boots, and a tall crowned hat with the brim turned up on one side, garnished with a pheasant feather. Indeed, with his trimmed beard and mustache, he struck a fashionable pose.

"And here, signore," said the servant, bowing, "is your dress sword. Do you wish to carry it, or shall I hand it to you at the church?"

"I will carry it—thank you. I believe it is time to join the others."

He descended the staircase and found the three ladies waiting, all in fine dresses of silk and satin. "You are indeed lovely, Mother," he said, kissing her on the cheek. "And you as well, Signora Elise." He kissed her hand, making a slight bow in the French manner. "And you, Aunt Caterina." She stood so stiffly that he settled for a pat on her shoulder. Her eyebrows shot up, but he lacked the desire to figure out why—not today, not when all his thoughts centered on the lady he loved with all his heart.

"And where are my uncle and future brother-in-law?" Stefano asked, looking around.

"Matteo was kind enough to go himself to fetch Etienne in the carriage," said his mother. She lowered her voice and added, "How handsome and distinguished you look, Son."

"He is late, though," said Signora Elise. "Etienne still must dress when he arrives."

At that moment, Uncle Matteo entered with a rapid pace from the side door. He went directly to Signora Elise and took both her hands in his. "It seems that Etienne has a fever. I found him in the factory infirmary. Don't worry. He is getting good care."

"But should he not be brought here? He will want his mother to care for him," said Signora Elise, her face white with anxiety.

"I left orders to bring him here the first thing in the morning—if his fever has not broken. I don't think it is anything grave. I spoke with him myself. While we are at the church, our servants will be busy preparing the betrothal meal and cannot look after him. And you will want to be with Françoise, will you not?"

"Of course. I accept your decision," she said limply. "I worry when one of my children is ill."

"Of course you do," said Stefano. *Why wouldn't she worry? She has lost four of her children as well as her husband—though not to illness.* The scene of the three struck by plague here in Milan crossed his mind. He wondered if Françoise had alerted her mother of the threat. This was certainly not the time to mention it, however. His uncle said the fever was not serious. It could be from any number of causes.

"I told the nursemaid to give Etienne special attention. And she will," said Uncle Matteo.

"Thank you."

"Shall we be off? This is a momentous day—my nephew is to pledge himself to marry." Uncle Matteo patted Stefano on his back, and the group went out to the awaiting coach.

&

A few family friends stood near the huge bronze doors of the Duomo to welcome Signora Elise, Stefano, and the other Marinellis when their coach arrived. Stefano was familiar with the custom. The betrothal ceremony would take place here, and afterward the party would enter the sanctuary to attend regular services.

Stefano stood nervously with the others waiting the arrival of Françoise in the Maffei carriage. To keep his mind occupied, he studied the bas-reliefs on the bronze doors, stories of saints and the history of Milan. His father had brought him here as a boy and explained the narratives. Little did he imagine then that one day he would stand on this very spot and pledge his love to his future wife.

The chatter of those around him suddenly stopped. He looked up and saw her. Françoise glowed with youthful beauty. Her hair, braided and wound as always in a bun high on her crown, was embellished with sprigs of rosemary. The collar of her dress, the sleeves, and the primary skirt were of pale pink silk. The bodice—pointed at the waist—and split overskirt were of velvet in a deeper rose. And she wore his short string of pearls around her lovely neck.

Her mother had already gone out to meet her and now walked on her right side, Lucrezia and Ferdinando on her left. Maria—with her hair braided in a bun—and Luca, both grinning and beautifully attired, walked in front.

The priest, a small wizened man with wisps of hair as white as his robe, suddenly appeared in the entranceway. The bronze doors now stood wide open. When all had gathered, he said in a loud voice, "Before all else, let those who are to be promised for future marriage come before the doors of the church." The couple joined hands and stood solemnly in front of him.

In a lower tone, the priest asked, "Do you, Stefano Marinelli and Françoise Chaplain, mutually consent to this betrothal?"

Stefano smiled at Françoise, eager to say aloud the confirming words. Together they said, "We do."

Stefano repeated after the priest, "Françoise, I fully intend to take you to be my wife, to espouse you. And I commit to you the fidelity and loyalty of my body and my possessions; and I will keep you in health and sickness and in any condition it shall please our Lord that you should have, nor for worse or for better will I change toward you until the end."

Françoise was asked to repeat the same with the extra promise of being "meek and obedient."

Next in order came the "blessing of the ring at the door of the church."

Stefano took a ring, which he had been wearing on his smallest finger, and held it up while the priest pronounced a blessing. Stefano then gave the invocation: "In the name of the Father." He placed the ring on Françoise's right thumb. "And of the Son." He removed it and placed it on her index finger. "And of the Holy Spirit." He now placed the ring on her fourth finger. "Amen." Then he added the words:

> "With this ring I promise thee to wed.
>   This gold and silver I thee give.
> With my body I thee worship,
>   And with my possessions I thee endow."

The priest asked, "Do the families have tokens of exchange?"

Uncle Matteo stepped forward with Aunt Caterina and his mother. "The Marinelli family offers this lute, symbol of the mutual love of music in both our families."

Signora Elise held out an embroidered tablecloth with a strand of red yarn pinned to it. "The Chaplains offer this gift, symbol of the threads of unity between the two families."

Stefano immediately realized that the strand of yarn must be the one Françoise had used to mark the days on her string of pearls—a symbol of her willingness to wait for him and of fidelity.

The priest said then, "The church recognizes and blesses this commitment. I now pronounce you betrothed to each other and to no other. You may seal this commitment with a kiss."

All stood in silence—with the exception of a giggle from Luca—while Stefano held Françoise's hands and placed his lips lovingly on hers. He felt her yield to him, her soft lips responding to his. They now belonged forever to each other.

When they turned around, Françoise's gaze darted among the witnesses. "Where is Etienne?"

"He is not feeling well," said her mother. "He only has a fever."

"He said to give you his best wishes," said Signore Matteo. "He is being well cared for at the factory infirmary. I saw him this morning, and he does not appear seriously ill."

"That is good," Françoise said with reservation.

Parishioners began arriving for the morning service, and the betrothal party entered the church along with them. Françoise took Stefano's arm. She looked into his eyes, but clouding her unspoken love was the thought of *plague*.

eighteen

At the Marinelli villa, Stefano joined the men assembled in the grand salon and talked of business. A group of twenty-one people had gathered for the betrothal celebration, including the priest and the guests present at the ceremony. The gala dinner would not be served until midafternoon. Uncle Matteo entertained by playing the lute given in the gift exchange. Although the families had presented token gifts to each other, the items would belong to the betrothed couple.

"I'm having another lute made for myself," said Uncle Matteo. "I wanted Françoise to have this one, for she plays as well as I, and Stefano enjoys listening to her."

"I think your nephew could *not* have chosen better," remarked one of his guests.

Stefano beamed when his uncle responded, "Thank you, signore. We consider her a gift from God."

❧

In the smaller salon, the women's conversation centered around marriage advice to Françoise. Much of it she found absurd or embarrassing, but that was the intent, according to tradition. Luca and Maria had gone with a twelve-year-old girl to another room to play games.

"Don't take that 'meek and obedient' part of the ceremony too seriously," said a guest. "There are methods of getting your own way." The woman winked and chuckled.

Stefano is the most patient man on the earth, Françoise thought. *I cannot imagine his being harsh or demanding.*

"And how many of God's little blessings do you hope to have, signorina?" probed another guest.

"Do you mean children?" she answered, trying to sound pleasant but failing. "We have not discussed that."

134

Lucrezia quickly turned the conversation to a new focus. "Why don't we each think of a favorite and pleasant story from our own marriages to share with Françoise?"

They all agreed, leaving the bride-to-be much relieved and pleased that Lucrezia had shown concern for her discomfort.

As the last lady related her story, Mira arrived to call them to the betrothal dinner. Françoise pulled her mother aside and lingered behind their guests. "Mamma, I am sorry I sounded rude. I know they were just seeking entertainment, and I should have heartily joined in, but I am so concerned about Etienne."

"As am I. Signore Matteo assured me he will receive good care, and one of the managers will bring him here in the morning if his fever has not broken."

"I have not had an opportunity to tell you, Mamma." Her face blanched with worry. "Stefano and I saw bodies being carried to a cart. The seeds of plague may have fallen on Milan."

Although Françoise suspected this news confirmed her mother's own fears, she took comfort in her response. "Signore Matteo would have brought him home immediately if he suspected serious illness. Let us stop in the chapel and place dear Etienne in the hands of the Lord." They stayed a few minutes in prayer, then, renewed in spirit, joined their guests in the dining hall.

સ

The multicourse dinner—which included ravioli made of herbs, chopped pork, roasted veal, cream cheese in a thin pastry, rendered fat, fried and rolled in powdered sugar—lasted three hours. Françoise joined in the light mood that prevailed. Servants pushed back the furniture and transformed the grand salon into a ballroom.

Stefano took Françoise's hand and led her to the center of the room. The others followed. Three hired musicians struck up a lively tune. Françoise felt she truly belonged to Stefano now, and she could see their committed love glowing in his face, reflecting her own happiness. They swirled about in each other's arms. For a few splendid hours, she forgot Etienne's illness and reveled in their mutual joy.

After the dancing, the guests went their separate ways. The Maffei family and Françoise left for home in their carriage. Stefano followed on horseback. He would begin his journey back to Florence in the morning. She would have only a few precious moments alone with her betrothed. On the morrow, she would return to her duties and her mother to hers, and Signore Matteo would set out on a trip to Genoa. Life would resume its normal routine—all infused with the new happiness of two families united.

৵

Stefano lit two torches in the Maffeis' enclosed garden, because by now night had fallen. A full moon added its light, and the couple found the outdoor air refreshing. He pulled Françoise beside him on the bench by the flagstone path that diagonally divided the area and overlooked the neatly trimmed hedges and blooming early-summer flowers.

"I am very happy to be promised to you," said Françoise. "You have been ever so patient with me—more than most men would have been."

"True, but I never doubted this day would come." He took her hand and kissed it. "You will be more secure now. But I am eager for us to be husband and wife. It is not good to be apart. When I am with you, my faith is stronger, and every day has more meaning."

"I wish you didn't have to leave in the morning, but I know you have no choice."

"I must do everything possible to move up at the bank so that we can establish our household, which will include our mothers and Etienne. Uncle Matteo has promised us a large sum of money when we marry. But it will only be enough, with my savings, to purchase a small house, not sufficient to sustain all of us."

"Your uncle is a good man, Stefano. But I think Signora Caterina, though never spiteful, still resents me."

"I haven't observed that, but I know she thinks highly of your mother." *How can anyone who knows her not adore Françoise?* he wondered.

"I finally told Mamma about what we saw—the dead bodies being put in the cart. I should have told her sooner. I pray Etienne is not sick with the plague. If he comes home before you leave in the morning, tell him how I love him."

"I will do so, Françoise."

She leaned her head on his shoulder. "I feel so safe when you are with me. But I sense a cloud of misfortune approaching." She shivered. "I love you, Stefano."

❦

The next morning, Stefano didn't wish to leave his uncle's villa before Etienne came home. But by the time the sun stood well above the horizon, he decided he must not linger. "They were to bring him *only* if he still had the fever, so he must have improved," he said, trying to reassure Signora Elise.

"I only wish I knew." She sighed and forced a smile.

"Do not worry, Signora Elise. I will check on him myself as I go out of town and send you a letter back," said Uncle Matteo. "I need to stop by my silk factory and speak with the managers anyway."

Assured that his uncle would see to Etienne, Stefano made his adieu at the same time, and the two men departed on their separate ways.

Later in the day, a carriage pulled up at the Marinelli gate. A servant rushed in to announce that Signore Matteo had returned and was carrying young Etienne to the house. The boy lay gravely ill.

❦

In a few days, Stefano arrived in Florence and reported to the bank at the usual morning hour. Much to his surprise, he found the writing stands and shelves of documents where he worked in disarray. They had been taught to keep everything neat and in order. And where were the other fellows? He thought he was quite alone until he spied Alessandro at a table in the corner poring over ledgers.

When he approached his master, Alessandro glanced up at him, then returned to his work. "So you are back," he growled.

Startled at this reception, so unlike Alessandro, Stefano answered, "Was not this the date, signore, that we were to return? And what is the cause of this disorder?"

"If you had returned yesterday, as did your fellow apprentices, you would have known about the discrepancies in some of your ledgers. These are petty clients, but, nonetheless, the total amount of missing funds is considerable." Alessandro never looked up as he made the charge.

Baffled, Stefano sat down across from Alessandro and waited. After several minutes, the master looked up and frowned. Stefano then spoke. "I have a right to defend myself, signore, whatever the charges. I assure you I have done nothing dishonorable. Of what am I accused? And by whom?"

"My secretary will be here shortly. We have been working on gathering the evidence over the past week," said Alessandro, looking down and shuffling his papers. "We do not seek a trial at this point. A scandal within the bank would not sit well with our major clients. Frankly, the loss of three well-trained apprentices would be our greatest blow. But we cannot tolerate dishonest clerks. Now if—"

"Three?" Stefano leaned across the table and again waited for Alessandro to look up. "Are you saying Diego and Luigi are implicated?"

"I am confirming nothing." Alessandro stood and faced Stefano. "You have been an excellent student, Stefano. I hope you can clear your name, but someone is to blame, and that someone's activities reflect badly on me as your—rather that someone's—supervisor. You are dismissed for the day, but be here promptly tomorrow morning. And don't touch any papers on the way out. Good day."

"Good day, signore. I ask only that you not make judgment until I have had the opportunity to prove my innocence."

With a slight bow, Stefano turned and left the room.

He wandered the streets of Florence on foot, pondering this new state of affairs. It was nothing like the return he had imagined. On the journey, he had turned words over in his mind of how he would announce his betrothal. Despite joking about Alessandro with his friends, he carried a fondness for the old gentleman. He had felt assured that his master would rejoice at his new commitment. Hadn't he said that married bankers were more trustworthy? He could expect Luigi and Diego to scoff, but he knew they would envy him. Now he would not so much as bring up the subject.

After hours of aimless walking, he started across the Santa Trinita Bridge but stopped halfway. He could view much of the city from here: the gigantic dome of Florence's Duomo, the fabulous Uffizi and Pitti palaces, magnificent public buildings, churches, statues, and fountains. He loved Florence and wanted to bring Françoise here. But if he were dismissed? He would have to start all over again, probably apprenticed to his uncle to become a merchant. How distasteful! And he would have to return to Françoise in disgrace.

He continued across the Arno River and on, until he came to a monastic church, Santo Spirito. He entered and gazed in reverence at the interplay of arches that gave the impression of tremendous depth. He knelt on the bare floor and prayed: *Father in heaven, forgive me for straying from Your worship. Keep Françoise safe and heal Etienne. And help me, O Lord, to clear my name of unjust charges. Lead me in the way I should go, for You are "the Rock that is higher than I."*

He strolled among the slender, gray stone columns and stopped at many of the elegant side altars, trying in this holy place to find peace and direction. Finally, he left and headed back toward his boardinghouse, stopping on the way to partake of a meal, alone, at a small tavern.

nineteen

By midweek, Françoise had heard nothing about Etienne's condition nor received a letter from Stefano. That, she knew, was to be expected. Stefano would not write until after he arrived back in Florence. Rarely did she receive any communication from her mother or the Marinellis. Yet anxiety hung over her, even as she tutored the children.

A servant tapped at the door. "Someone is here to see you, signorina—"

She jumped up with alarm, letting the teaching materials fall from her lap. Could it be a message from Stefano or her mother? Good news? Bad news?

"His name is Filippo, and he says he comes from the Grand Duke of Tuscany. He says you should have some letter for him. Do you wish—?"

Françoise dropped back in her chair and picked up the fallen papers. "The letter he seeks is on the writing stand shelf in the grand salon. You may hand it to him and say, 'With regards from Françoise Chaplain.' I do not wish to see him— but don't say that. If he insists, then you may call on me. Thank you."

"Yes, signorina. As you wish."

❧

On Sunday, Françoise hoped Signore Matteo would send a carriage for her. She never knew in advance but always anticipated its arrival until the usual time had passed. Late in the morning, well past the time, she changed from her church attire to her regular housedress. Nervous and agitated, she flitted from needlework to Scripture reading in the chapel to pacing about her room. Late in the afternoon, a servant knocked on her door to announce that a man awaited her at the front gate. She rushed out to find Signore Matteo alone on his horse, no carriage. He dismounted as she approached.

As she drew nearer, her heart sank. His face spoke only grief. She had seen that look on other faces and felt it on her own. He stood well back from the gate, the vertical bars effacing strips of his image. She placed her hands on the bars and felt imprisoned. "Signore Matteo, what is wrong?" The words choked in her throat.

"I'm sorry, Françoise." His voice cracked like an elderly person's.

"It's Etienne, my precious little brother?"

Signore Matteo nodded.

"He suffered terribly, didn't he?"

Signore Matteo looked down. Françoise broke into uncontrollable sobs. She pressed her face so tightly against the gate that it bruised her flesh, and she clung to the iron bars until her fingers turned white. She thrust her arm through the gate and cried out, "Hold my hand, Signore Matteo. I need your comfort."

He shook his head. "I can't. I come from a house the plague has visited. I'm breaking the law by coming here."

"My mother!"

"Your mother is sick. But you must not come to her. No one must enter the house. We will do all that can be done."

"But I must be with her!" she sobbed. "She needs me to be there."

"She told me to tell you not to come."

"She wouldn't tell me that!" Françoise bawled out like a cow giving birth. "She wouldn't say not to come."

Signore Matteo slowly mounted his horse and, without looking back, rode away.

Françoise hung on the gate, crying aloud. Time passed. Finally, her sobs diminished to silent jerks of her exhausted body. Her hands ached as she slowly let go of her grip on the bars. She wiped her eyes with her sleeve, not even bothering to take out her handkerchief. With head lowered, she trudged back to the house. Where was God? She could not bring herself to prayer.

Lucrezia and a maidservant had stood watching at a front window. Lucrezia opened the door and took her into her arms. She held her close and patted her back. "There, there," she said. "What did he tell you?"

The maid stood frozen in place, staring at the two red impressions of bars streaking down Françoise's face. "Well, bring us some hot herbal tea," said Lucrezia. The maid hurried off.

Françoise slumped into a chair and pulled out her handkerchief. She blew her nose. "Etienne is dead," she whispered hoarsely.

"From the fever?"

She nodded. "The plague."

Lucrezia stepped back, dropping her tone of sympathy. "You cannot bring the seeds of the plague into this house."

Françoise sat up straight. "Didn't you see? Signore Matteo stood well back from the gate. He brought Etienne home the day *after* we left. You are safe!" She spit out the last words, angry that her friend would be more concerned about herself than sharing her sorrow.

"I saw."

The maid brought a kettle and cups, set them on a table, bowed, and then dismissed herself. The tea sat cooling and untouched.

"My mother is ill. I must go to her."

"No, Françoise, you must not." Lucrezia's voice was softer but still calculating. "No one is to enter a house of plague. It is the law."

"I must go to Mamma. She needs me."

"If you go, you cannot return to this house."

Françoise began weeping again.

"Come," said Lucrezia, helping Françoise to her feet. "You need to rest." She assisted her upstairs to her room. Like a maidservant, Lucrezia loosened her clothing and helped her into a nightgown. Françoise fell limply onto the bed and closed her eyes. "I order you *not* to leave this house."

No sooner had the door closed behind Lucrezia than Françoise began to moan in grief. She tossed about, blaming herself for Etienne's death. *I should have told Mother and everyone immediately when I knew the plague had come to Milan. Perhaps Signore Matteo would have allowed Etienne to remain at home if he had known it was a threat. They say that one should stay away from crowded places—like factories. I should have done something to prevent this.*

Mercifully, she fell into a deep sleep. She dreamed of Etienne and her father returning from a successful fishing trip. They smelled of fish and the sea. They were laughing and bragging about their good catch. Then she was playing with her three young siblings, dressing the baby on her lap while the toddler and the older ones chased each other around her chair. Suddenly the house was burning, and the little ones cried out to her to save them.

She awoke with a start. In real life, she had never heard their screams, but they seemed so real now. She had not saved any of them, nor Etienne. Questions she should have asked of Signore Matteo came to mind. When did he die? Did he have a funeral and a decent burial?

The sun had set, and dusk was falling by the time a maid brought a bowl of soup and bread. She sat up and ate mechanically. *I must go to my mother. She needs me.*

She set the unfinished bowl aside and slowly began to devise a plan. Though the room was now in total darkness, she didn't light a lamp for fear it would be detected. Slipping on the dress she had worn that day, she crept downstairs and out the side door. Unlike the other doors with keys, this one opened with a latch from the inside. She closed it as quietly as possible and heard the latch click into place. It might well be her own death knell. Lucrezia had said she could not return.

The streets lay quiet and deserted. Her footsteps echoed on the cobblestones. She should have brought a lantern. Thick fog hung in layers and made walking difficult—as though she were blind. Her sense of direction told her when she had arrived at Via Padova. She turned left. Early dawn brought diffused light, and she could see shapes of houses and trees through the eerie haze.

The clatter of rapidly approaching horses' hooves frightened her, but the coach passed, giving her no mind. Before long, other vehicles emerged through the fog, all coming toward her, all moving swiftly as if being chased. *Where are they going?*

By the time Françoise arrived at the villa gate, sun had pierced the fog in shafts of light. A wooden panel hung on one of the wide stone gateposts. Up close she could see a large red cross had been painted thereupon—a sign of the plague. And underneath she made out the words: "Lord, have mercy on us." When she was a child, her grandmother had told her stories of plague-ridden cities. Houses were forced to be labeled thus to keep the family locked in and others out.

Coaches and carriages continued to rumble down the street, all going in the same direction. Now she could see they were laden with goods of every sort, even furniture. A servant woman carrying a large basket hurried along at the side of the street. Françoise called out to her. The woman recoiled. "Do you come from the plague-ridden house?" she asked.

"No, I have not been inside. Do you know where everyone is going?"

The woman cackled a humorless laugh. "They're leaving. Those who have the means are getting out of town. Going anywhere they have relatives or friends. The poor are left to die in their houses. Of course, *these* rich folks got caught by surprise." She waved her hand toward the villa. "My mistress has sent me to the markets to lay in all the supplies we can." The woman hurried on her way, throwing a warning over her shoulder, "Don't go in that plague-house."

Françoise breathed in deeply, took courage, and pulled the bell rope. After several minutes, she rang again, more persistently. By the third time, she saw a young man materializing in the mists. It was Sergio, the stable hand.

"Signorina Françoise," he whispered. "I'll call someone. Wait here."

She waited for perhaps half an hour, pacing back and forth. Finally, she stood facing the street and watched the frantic traffic.

"Is that you, Françoise?"

She turned to face a disheveled woman, hollow eyed, her long hair hanging loose. The dark eyebrows, slightly lifted, told Françoise this must be none other than Signora Caterina. The woman stopped a good distance from the gate.

"Oh, Signora Caterina, you have endured so much!" For the first time, Françoise realized the pain of the others in the house.

"Thank you for coming, Françoise. We are prisoners here. To see your face brings a small measure of comfort." She pulled a shawl tightly around herself and trembled.

Françoise noticed a rosy ring of petal-shaped blotches on her sunken cheeks. "You, too, are ill. Oh, Signora Caterina!"

"I prayed you would come. There is so much I want to say before I die."

Silent tears ran down Françoise's face. "I must go in and see my mother."

"Françoise, your mother is dead."

Somehow she already knew, but the words stung. "When? When did she die? I should have been here." She came close to the gate and clasped her fingers around the bars as before but did not press her face against them.

"No, you should not have been. Unlike the others, she slipped away as in sleep. But her last words to me were, 'Tell my daughter I have gone to be with her father and Etienne, my older son and the little ones. I see all their faces waiting for me. They are smiling and rejoicing to be with our Savior, Jesus Christ. Tell her not to come in this house. Though she will want to be with me, she must not. Give her my blessing.'

I remember every word just as she said it, for I was Elise's caregiver until the last.

"Then after a while your mother said, 'Stefano is a good man. Tell Françoise to love us all by loving him and to have children so that our families will live on.'" Then she turned her face to the wall. Only a little while later I checked on her, and she was cold."

"When? I must know when."

"Etienne passed away two days after he came home. She stayed at his side the whole time. Then she became ill and was already gone by the time Matteo came back from telling you about Etienne. Matteo had his workmen make a proper coffin as he had for your brother. Then they took her in the carriage to the churchyard. The sexton would not let us enter. We waited outside and watched them lower the casket into one of the freshly dug graves. A priest came out and prayed over her and some others. They were getting so many bodies—three or four a day—that they had begun to dig a pit as they did back in the epidemic of 1530. We had gone to the church for Etienne—he was one of the first in this neighborhood."

"Thank you, Signora Caterina, for telling me this. I needed to know." Her eyes were dry now. She treasured her mother's last words, but the pain inside her breast remained heavy as ever.

Fortunately, she had the presence of mind to ask, "And Matteo—your dear husband—has he. . . ?"

"He was already struck with the illness when he returned from the church burial. His was not easy like your mother's." Signora Caterina spoke without emotion, her grief long since beyond expression.

"May I bring you provisions?"

"That is not needed. Sergio sneaked out night before last, waited until dawn, then brought back goods from the market. The watchman never caught him." She coughed. "We have plenty in store. But the watchman passes by several times a day between our place and another down the street. No one is allowed to leave."

"Who is still left to care for you?"

"Isabella and Mira. They have not yet been stricken. Isabella was up all night caring for a servant who died. She is sleeping now. I will tell her you were here."

"Has word been sent to Stefano?"

"Isabella wrote a letter, but no one will take it. We plan to send Sergio on horseback as he is eager to get out of Milan. He cares for the animals and sleeps in the hay, refusing to come inside the house."

Françoise could see great beads of sweat on Signora Caterina's forehead even at the distance between them. "You must go in and rest, Signora Caterina. May God bless you and ease your pain. . . ." She sought words to thank her for caring for her mother, but they choked in her throat.

"One last word, Françoise." She took a small step forward. "Please know that I have always loved you, though I never properly expressed it. Like you, I feared trusting and loving. You are so like my daughter. We disapproved of the nobleman she wanted to marry, but Matteo and I finally gave in to her wishes." She paused to cough several times in a retching sort of way. "Our daughter never forgave us for trying to dissuade her. If you are ever in Rome, her name is Lydia Capello. They are a noble family of some standing. If you ever see her, tell her—" Signora Caterina broke into an uncontrollable cough.

"I will."

Signora Caterina waved awkwardly and staggered back toward the villa.

Françoise stood transfixed, not moving until the woman disappeared through the doorway. The fog had lifted into clouds that overcast the sky as Françoise wearily made her way back toward the only home she might still have.

❧

Françoise approached the house, remembering Lucrezia's words not to come back if she left. But of all the misfortunes, losing her home did not seem a major concern. She had not even prepared words of explanation. When she arrived at the gate, she could see Lucrezia standing at the window. She came out, rather than sending a servant, to the gate and stood at a distance.

Françoise saw anger clearly written across her face. "You dare to come back here?" accused Lucrezia. "You would bring death to my little ones. I told you not to go, so your fate is your own choosing. You must find other lodging."

"Lucrezia, I did not enter the Marinelli villa. Not even past the gate." Her voice sounded steady and firm, not begging for sympathy, but simply laying out the facts. "My mother is dead, and Signore Matteo as well. I talked with Signora Caterina at a distance."

"There are poisonous vapors in the air. You went out in the dead of night and breathed the night air and mingled with people on the street."

Françoise stood her ground, making no move to leave.

Lucrezia finally gave a deep sigh. "All right. I will unlock the gate. Wait awhile after I return to the house, then go around to the enclosed garden in back. I will unlatch that gate. Enter only after my maid has left you a tub of water and clothing. Bathe and wash your hair in the vinegar I leave there." Françoise guessed that Lucrezia had planned to relent in case she had not actually been in the villa. Her directions sounded well thought out. Lucrezia turned to go, then added, "And leave your clothing by the back wall to be burned. No one will see you naked as I will keep the children from the windows."

Françoise paced up and down by the gate. Though her legs ached from the long walk, moving renewed her energy. She knew how frightened Lucrezia must be. But in spite of her worry, Lucrezia had thought to ensure her privacy. *Try as she might, she cannot abandon her Christian charity and turn me away.*

When she felt enough time had lapsed, she made her way to the garden gate. Inside sat a tub of warm water and beside it her folded clothing with a slab of soap on top. She stripped and cleansed herself in the prescribed manner. Memories emerged of another time, another place, another woman frightened that she might carry the plague—dear Isabella, who took her in and became her friend. And that friend even now remained trapped inside the villa! She prayed God's mercy to rest upon her.

twenty

In Florence, Stefano rose early, trimmed his beard and mustache, dressed, and broke his fast with the other boarders. In a way, he missed Diego and Luigi, who were always good for a few laughs. He ate his bread and cheese in a corner by himself and thought through the events of the past two weeks.

All three apprentices had been taught the same penmanship, and thus it became difficult to distinguish one's figures from another's. Though they were to initial their work, Stefano's *SM* resembled very closely Luigi's *LM*. Some of the work Stefano said of a certainty was his, Luigi claimed as his. Documents with discrepancies were denied by both. Alessandro told Stefano that Diego and Luigi had explained that, since Stefano worked much faster than they, he had taken on some of their accounts. Certainly *SM* was affixed to nearly half of the work.

Finally, Stefano, desperate to clear his name, returned to the bank and called Alessandro aside. He told him of a conversation he recalled with both his counterparts. "One of them complained that they were not well enough paid, and the other said something about it being easy enough to make the ledgers add up to pay themselves more."

"And why did you not report this to me immediately, Stefano?" said Alessandro, looking perturbed. "I taught all of you that Cosimo de' Medici insists that loyalty to the bank be above all else, and that includes reporting any disloyalty."

"I know, signore. I apologize for failing to do so," said Stefano in all sincerity. "I put loyalty to my peers above loyalty to the Medici Bank. I regret that."

"And which young man made which statement?"

"I have tried to remember, but I cannot," said Stefano. "I do recall they looked knowingly at each other as though they had previously discussed it. I thought it was just something they were considering but did not yet dare to do."

With more study of the initials, Stefano discovered the forged *S* was slightly larger than Stefano's own hand. When Alessandro confronted Luigi with the stark evidence, he finally admitted he had done all the forging, but Diego had distorted numbers as much as he. Luigi had mistakenly thought his distant relationship to the Medicis would spare him.

But, along with Diego, he was immediately dismissed from the bank and Stefano retained. Stefano's relationship with his master, however, remained tense. Alessandro heard of his intention to marry through gossip and accused Stefano of keeping that information from him. Once Stefano let his betrothal be known by refusing an introduction to a prospective bride, he was no longer one of the most sought-after bachelors in Florentine society.

With the other two apprentices gone, Stefano's workload increased tremendously but not his salary. New apprentices had been hired, but they were months away from taking on responsible duties. He often found himself working in his room by lamplight to finish the day's business.

He worried about his future with the company, as any aspiring young man anticipating marriage might. Of course, Alessandro would not always be his master. As he moved up, he would report to others. Even with his name cleared, still a sense of suspicion might well hang over his head. Perhaps the Sforza Bank in Milan would take him on. But he so greatly admired the art and architecture in Florence, he hated to leave. His mother would prefer Milan. Where would Françoise be happiest?

These thoughts troubled him continually. But one late afternoon, six weeks after clearing his name, while he worked earnestly on an account, Alessandro asked to speak with him in private, whereupon he learned a decision had already been made for him.

"Stefano, please be seated. Your work here is commendable.

No one denies that. You are an asset to the company, but there has been a new turn of events."

Stefano showed no reaction but tried to prepare himself for dismissal.

"Filippo, whom you have seen from time to time around the bank, is the personal servant of Cosimo."

"Yes, signore, I am aware of that."

"Before I go much further, would you affirm or deny that this is your penmanship?" He handed Stefano a letter across the table.

Stefano immediately recognized the message Françoise had dictated to him in which she gave her betrothal as the reason for turning down Cosimo's offer of harpsichord lessons. His jaw dropped in shock. Several seconds later, he gained his composure. "Yes, I admit the penmanship is mine, and it is signed by my betrothed," he said in a straightforward manner.

"Filippo came here to see me this morning and loaned me this letter for your confirmation. It seems Cosimo recognized the handwriting as the style taught here and easily concluded you were the man who won the fair lady—over him. He deemed it an added insult that you wrote the letter. Filippo confided that Cosimo has not been well of late and spends his time shut up in a room where he forces scholars to read to him." Alessandro lowered his voice and looked around. "This information is not to be spread about as a rumor."

"It will remain safe with me, signore."

"Filippo told me he had waited some time before giving this letter to him, hoping to find the duke in a better temper. But finding him consistently sulky and daring not to wait longer, he delivered it to him. As it was sealed with wax, Filippo had no notion of the contents. Cosimo became enraged upon discovering he had been rebuffed for the second time by the same woman. According to Filippo, Cosimo had probably forgotten about your betrothed. . . . So her name is Françoise?" Alessandro smiled with approval.

Stefano nodded.

"He has plenty of women—as well as a new mistress in the palace whom he ignores. Though Cosimo had sent Filippo to obtain Françoise's response, he never asked for it. But now that Cosimo has seen the letter, he is furious. And this is the part I regret to tell you—"

"Does he wish to stab me through and through, as he did poor Almeni?" asked Stefano, partly in jest and partly in fear.

"No, no." Alessandro chuckled, then became more serious. "He could do that, of course. No, what Cosimo actually shouted was, 'Get that man, Stefano Marinelli, out of my bank and out of Florence!'"

Stefano rose to go. "I will leave immediately, signore."

"Sit down, son. I have not finished." Alessandro's eyes twinkled. "I've always liked you. Yet you peeved me by not telling me sooner about the untrustworthy Luigi and Diego. I have always enjoyed your interest in the great artists and architects of Florence. You do genuinely admire them, do you not?"

"Yes, of course."

"How would you like to join our branch bank in Rome? That city is in the midst of magnificent construction—wide streets and piazzas, statues and gardens. All the great artists are represented. You can watch the dome of St. Peter's Basilica go up, designed by the late Michelangelo himself. Obviously the need for banking has tremendously increased. The facilities of the branch bank are in the process of enlargement and need gifted young men conversant in the arts as well as investments. May I recommend you, Stefano?"

Stefano sat stunned. Before he could recover from the shock of being ousted from paradise, a much larger gate opened to him. Since he must leave Florence, then he should not hesitate to grab this new opportunity. "Yes, signore. Thank you. I would very much like to be recommended for Rome."

"Good. A representative of the Roman bank will be here this week. With my recommendation, your new position is assured. You may remain in town until I have arranged an interview for you, but stay out of sight. I assured Filippo you would be gone before sunset."

Both men stood and shook hands, and Stefano left with a lilt in his step.

❧

During his first week back in Florence, Stefano had written Françoise a brief note and sent it by a young man on his way to Milan. Being in the midst of accusations against him and not knowing the outcome, he avoided mentioning his problems. But, among other things, he wrote, "I assume Etienne is in good health, as he did not return home before I left." Also he asked Françoise to write to him. "I'm sure Ferdinando will be able to find someone suitable to deliver a letter in Florence."

Now several weeks had gone by with no word. He began to ask every day at the boardinghouse desk if perhaps he had a message. This afternoon the clerk handed him a small, but heavy, package. With much excitement, he rushed to his room to open it. But to his surprise and disappointment, he found his own letter enclosed and still sealed as well as the coins he had paid the messenger. He read the attached note:

> *Signore Marinelli,*
> *I journeyed no farther than Parma where I was informed that Milan has been struck by a vile contagion. I attempted to pass your letter on to a trusted traveler who seemed determined to return home to his family in that city. He refused to deliver it, however, not wishing to take the risk. From others at the inn, I learned that no messages or objects of any kind were allowed to pass into clean houses. Those marked with red crosses could receive but not send same. I have kept ten percent of the fee for my trouble and have enclosed the rest.*

Stefano dropped to his knees and poured out his heart to God with tears and trembling. How could he have left Françoise there, vulnerable to the plague? And his mother? And the others—what had become of them? In the back of his mind, he had convinced himself he had not seen the bodies being loaded into a cart that day. And if he had, there must be some other explanation. He had left Milan with his mind focused on earning a living for his new household. Everyone at the villa, even Françoise's mother, had encouraged him to be on his way that morning. "Etienne has probably recovered by now, or they would have brought him home." *Françoise could not bear to lose Etienne.*

He would leave in the morning. In little time, he stuffed his belongings into two bags. It was still daylight when he went out to the stables to feed his horse. He craved the exercise of walking or riding but knew he could not allow himself to be seen. What of the new position? He would leave a note for Alessandro explaining the circumstances of his abrupt departure. He lingered sometime around the stables before returning.

Dusk had fallen. The servants were already serving the evening meal of vegetable soup and bread. The steamy room reeked of sweat and overcooked carrots and cabbage. He sat in his accustomed corner and ate without tasting his food.

"Here. This came for you while you were out." The proprietor startled him by suddenly laying a folded and sealed paper by his bowl. The man walked away before Stefano could thank him, but he would not have been heard anyway over the loud talking in the crowded dining hall.

Slowly he opened the paper and saw it was from Alessandro. He read: "Our bank representative from Rome arrived just after you left. All is well. Meet us at the Blue Goose Tavern on the corner of your street at ten of the clock in the morning. Be ready to leave town immediately after signing papers."

For the sake of his future, logic dictated that he stay for the meeting in the morning. As he had no accounts to work on this evening, he remained in the dining hall and played a game of cards with some beer-quaffing fellows. He decided to wait until morning to apprise the proprietor of his departure. That way he could leave his baggage in his room until after the meeting.

❧

Though Stefano's mind was filled with worry, he felt the meeting with the Medici Bank representative from Rome went extremely well. The representative described the economic explosion in Rome and the beauty of the city. He seemed impressed with Stefano's congeniality, refinement, and knowledge—all drawn out by Alessandro. Stefano would be promoted to a more responsible position with double the salary. He would report to the bank in Rome on September one, six weeks from now.

With papers signed, Alessandro and the representative lingered to discuss the art and architecture of Rome. Stefano, though eager to be on his way, felt obliged to be an attentive listener. After a sufficient time, however, Stefano rose to thank his hosts.

"Just one more item, son," said Alessandro.

Stefano sat back down and leaned in to hear the lowered voice of his master.

"I heard from a good source this morning—but you must not repeat it—our Grand Duke of Tuscany, Cosimo de' Medici, was seized by an apoplectic fit just last evening. They say it was his second attack; the first was kept secret. This time he has lost the use of his arms and legs. And his voice! He sits mumbling incoherently."

"How does this affect the Medici Bank?" asked the representative.

"Not at all, I would think," said Alessandro. "He has paid us little attention the past few years."

Stefano was relieved that his new position remained intact. He folded his copy of the contract, tucked it inside his doublet, shook hands, and thanked his hosts. He walked briskly to the boardinghouse on Via delle Oche, eager to head back to Milan.

twenty-one

Ferdinando Maffei's mule train remained idle. Françoise knew that, like most merchants, he could be ruined financially. No one in Milan was buying any goods that were not absolutely necessary. No one outside the city would buy anything coming from Milan.

For several days, Lucrezia kept the children from Françoise, not convinced of their safety. Françoise stayed in her room, eating little, praying, and crying. The children, with nothing constructive required of them, quarreled and fought much of the time. Françoise could hear Lucrezia and Ferdinando arguing over insignificant issues.

All servants had abandoned them—except one woman—leaving much of the upkeep of garden, animals, and house to the Maffeis themselves. Like many others, their servants feared that if they stayed and the plague struck, they would be trapped like prisoners, forced to care for the sick, and would die themselves.

Finally, Lucrezia tapped on Françoise's door.

"You may come in, Lucrezia."

She entered and sat in the only chair. Françoise rose from her bed, where she had been lying and weeping, and sat on its edge.

"My husband and I talked last night," she began with hesitation. Françoise thought she was about to be thrown out into the streets—though the idea did not disturb her. Life could hardly become more miserable. "We believe that to preserve our sanity and that of the children, we should return to a semblance of daily routine. Are you able, Françoise, to tutor the children as before?"

"You are the one who insisted on my isolation," Françoise

said with bitterness. She dried her eyes and blew her nose. "But you are right—routine would be good for us all. Otherwise we will turn crazy and bring destruction on each other. I will meet Luca and Maria in their study room within the hour."

&

Thus Françoise felt the situation inside the Maffei house improved somewhat. Together they made a list of all necessary chores with names attached to each. The woman servant became equal to the others, or rather they all equally became servants. The children's mother assigned them light household tasks, and Françoise asked them to help with the small vegetable garden beside the house. Ferdinando took care of the horses and one cow and made an effort to trim the enclosed garden. Lucrezia helped with the cooking, which, of necessity, became rather creative.

They ate no fresh meat during the entire confinement. Vegetables had been planted early in the season only to supplement those from the market; thus the garden offered scant variety to their meals. Fortunately, the cellar and storeroom were well stocked with cheese and flour for bread.

Françoise took up the lute that Signore Matteo had presented at the betrothal ceremony. She played and sang the psalms that had always given her comfort. It brought none, but she felt closer to her mother and brother by doing so. Gradually the others joined her and sang along. She composed a few children's songs by incorporating the lessons into music. Luca and Maria found this amusing, which provided a small measure of pleasure to Françoise.

Rather than a sense of security and well-being, Françoise felt the emotions of this isolated group were more akin to those of a person clinging to a raft in the midst of a turbulent sea, at each moment expecting to succumb to the crashing waves about him.

Although everyone made an effort to protect the children from the horrors around them, the adults often found themselves at the front windows, mesmerized by the drama taking place in the street. Unlike the two crosses Françoise remembered from the Marinelli neighborhood, plenty of houses here bore the warning sign.

Every day, she observed, some of those tormented by the plague escaped from their houses and ran shrieking down the street. Some were overcome with delusions and claimed to see terrible visions before them. "Rakers" collected thrown-out, infected bedding and trash and burned it in the streets. The front windows were kept sealed, but in the heat of August, the back ones were opened—allowing the stench to drift in.

Most terrible of all was the sound of the bell announcing the approach of the dead carts. The man ringing it led a horse pulling the cart. A burier or two would collect the bodies brought out of the infected houses. Or they would pick up those who had died alone in the streets. A few mourners followed silently or with loud laments. The bodies were to be thrown into a huge pit in the churchyard between sunset and sunrise.

Françoise watched and thanked God that her loved ones had, at least, received a decent Christian burial. *But where is Stefano? Does he know? Did he stay in Florence to protect himself? I cannot blame him for that. But how I need him!* Absently, she twisted the ring of betrothal on her finger.

❧

Stefano's concerns over what he would find in a few days back in Milan greatly overshadowed his pleasure of moving up in the world. He knew it possible that all his loved ones were spared. The plague usually ravished the slum districts to a greater extent. Those better off would have more provisions in store and could wait out the epidemic—or leave the city. Uncle Matteo could not send him word unless he did so illegally.

He mounted the few steps to the boardinghouse and opened the door. He walked directly into the dining area, where a clerk usually sat behind a counter at the side. Coming in from the bright sun, he perceived the room to be entirely empty and dashed toward the stairs that led to his room.

"Buon giorno, Signore Marinelli."

He followed the voice to a young man sitting at one of the tables.

"Sergio!" The servant stood, and the two embraced. "You have come from Milan. Tell me everything."

"Both our mothers live. That is the good news."

"Thank the good Lord for that. And Uncle Matteo and Aunt Caterina? Signora Elise and Etienne?"

"All dead. All the servants have died or deserted the villa," said Sergio. "There are only the three of us left. My mother, Mira, and Signora Isabella. I am sorry."

Stefano hadn't known the head servant, Mira, was Sergio's mother. He should have known, having lived for some time at his uncle's villa. His grief over the loss of his relatives and increased concern over Françoise swept over him. He ran his fingers through his hair and groaned. He feared asking but did: "And Françoise Chaplain? The Maffei household?"

"We have heard nothing. Much of the better side of town was only lightly struck—the villa near us and ours were the only two in our neighborhood. Many of the wealthy left town. The others knew to stay indoors and take precautions."

"Did Françoise ever come back to the villa—to see Etienne and her mother?" *She could have picked up the seeds of the plague.*

"Yes, she came but not indoors. I answered the gate myself." Sergio sighed, hesitating to say the sorrowful words again. "Both were already dead. I would have come here sooner, but your mother feared I would bring the contagion to you. She said to tell you not to come before cold weather, when the disease should subside."

"I plan to leave for Milan as soon as I pick up my baggage," Stefano said with determination. "Will you go back with me?"

"Mother told me to stay and seek my fortune in Florence, to hire myself as an apprentice to a trade. I had planned to do so. But if you have the courage to return, then I will go with you!" exclaimed Sergio with a pound of his fist on the table.

Stefano suspected Sergio feared striking out on his own as much as the plague.

He was glad for Sergio's company, and the two began the journey of several days back to Milan. They rode side by side on horseback. Stefano had never experienced the services of a personal servant, with the exception of a few rare occasions on loan from Uncle Matteo. Sergio had been Uncle Matteo's house servant, then stable hand, but not *his*. Thus the two traveled comfortably as equals.

During the journey, Stefano wanted to know the details of the more recent days in the Marinelli household to prepare himself.

"No one has sickened and died in several weeks," said Sergio. "One servant woman did recover and begged Signora Isabella to release her, which she did. I took care of feeding and exercising the horses. Mother and Signora Isabella scoured the rooms with soap and vinegar. I carried the infected bedding from the house to the street, where the rakers set it on fire. The women aired out the house and burned rosin and pitch all day to sweeten the rooms.

"The watchman officially took down the red-cross warning and departed from our street. Before Signora Isabella finally released me to go to Florence, she asked me to sell all the horses except those needed to pull the family carriage. With the plague virtually gone in this part of the city, I was able to sell them for not much below normal prices. To make the last purchase of vegetables before leaving, I rode out of town to buy directly from farmers and away from the crowds."

"Do you have any idea of how widespread the plague was throughout the city—how many died?" asked Stefano.

"Now that I was free to wander about, I stopped by the Duomo to check the bills of mortality that were posted weekly. Once before, on one of my rare clandestine trips for provisions, I had noted nearly three hundred names posted that week for this parish alone. But the day before I left, there were only twelve parish deaths, plus a bishop and three other dignitaries. I guess throughout the city thousands died."

They rode along in silence while Stefano pondered the catastrophe his loved ones had endured.

As they approached Milan, Sergio told him, "We must purchase our provisions on the outskirts, for as we pass through the slums, we should stop for nothing. And we must bind cloths stuffed with spices about our mouths and noses to guard against the foul air."

"I will follow your advice, Sergio."

They bought the spices and some fruit and bread and filled their water flasks, then donned the masks and rode ahead.

Stefano braced himself against whatever horrors they might encounter.

But when they arrived, he realized how ill prepared he was for the extent of human misery. The muddy streets were filled with filth of every sort. A nauseous odor like rotting fish filled his nostrils, even through the protective filter. Groans, wails, and curses seemed to come in waves as if orchestrated.

As they passed a butcher's shop, Stefano noted with curiosity that the few customers took the meat they wished to purchase from the hooks themselves, then dropped their coins into a jar of liquid as the merchant watched. "What are they doing, Sergio? What is the liquid?"

"Only vinegar. The merchant will not touch the money until it is cleansed."

As they watched, a man who had just made a purchase fell sprawling to the ground, his leg of lamb on top of his chest. The poor man writhed and raved in agony, clutching the bloody meat, as a few patrons watched. Others walked by without paying any mind.

Stefano halted his horse, as did Sergio.

"It's his groin," explained Sergio, shaking his head. "When the swellings become hard and refuse to burst, the agony is unbearable."

"Cannot something be done?"

At that moment, Stefano noticed that a handbarrow had

been sitting in front of the shop for just such an occasion. A bearer hauled the screaming fellow into it and rolled him down the street.

"They won't bury him alive, will they?" Stefano asked with shock.

"No, though I hear that has happened," said Sergio. "They are taking him to a pest-house, where a nurse will attempt to lay a poultice on the bubo, as the swelling is called. Or they may burn it with caustics. He might even recover."

They moved on hurriedly. Stefano witnessed a dead man being robbed of his money, poor people lined up at fortune-tellers, and hawkers of remedies of every sort. He steered his horse around a body lying in his path.

Late in the day, they passed the Duomo and turned down the Via Padova. Whereas the slums had been crowded with people, here the street was nearly deserted. The quietness came as a relief, but it was the sort of stillness that precedes a storm—uncertain and foreboding. The boarded-up houses and overgrown gardens spoke of death, also. Stefano feared finding his mother dead at the villa.

He rang the bell at the gate. Within a few minutes, both his mother and Mira emerged from the front entrance and ran to open the gate. With tears streaming down their faces, they embraced their sons. To Stefano, his mother appeared older and less plump but most certainly alive.

"I wish I had stayed with you to go through this trial," he said, kissing both her cheeks. "But, thank God, you and Mira live!"

Sergio returned to his servant role and took the horses to the stables. Stefano, with an arm around each woman, walked back to the villa.

"Neither of you was to come back here," said Mira. "But our joy overflows to see you."

"Yes," said his mother. "I cannot scold you for disobeying. For after all our misery, your presence overcomes us with happiness. We have cleansed the house of the plague. Come in."

Night had fallen by the time the little group finished a simple meal that included some of the fruit the young men had purchased outside Milan.

"Have you received any word from Françoise?" Stefano finally asked with dread in his heart. His mother had said nothing, which led him to expect the worst.

"Stefano, I wish I could give you an answer—a good answer," she said with hesitancy showing in her voice. "But, to tell you the truth, we do not know anything. It has been two months since Françoise came here to our gate. That is when Caterina told her of the deaths of Etienne and her mother. We have heard nothing since."

"And no one went to inquire?" Stefano heard accusation in his own voice. "No, I don't mean you should have. I saw the horrors you must have endured when we rode through the slums."

"We hear no news at all," said Mira. "So the plague still rages in some parts of the city?"

"You didn't stop, did you, going through those streets?" asked his mother in alarm.

"No," said Sergio. "We wore masks and touched nothing."

"Do you still have a carriage and horses?" asked Stefano. "I must go for Françoise early tomorrow morning."

"Yes, Son, that is exactly what you must do—fetch Françoise."

❧

Stefano left in the carriage as dawn was breaking through the cypress trees in long shafts of sunlight. The deserted Via Padova of boarded-up houses soon gave way to evidences of still-active plague. He passed an empty dead cart coming from the churchyard and piles of filth burning in the streets. Few people were about besides the city watchmen whose job it was to keep the quarantine of infected houses in force. He noticed an occasional house marked with the red cross. The telltale odors of rotting fish and pungent vinegar filled the air. *Almighty God*, he prayed as he pulled up to the house gate, *may it have pleased You to spare the life of Françoise. . . .*

After stepping down from the carriage, Stefano rang the bell and waited a short while. He looked up and saw a woman walking rapidly toward him from the house. With the morning sun behind her, he could not be sure of her identity. Her dark hair hung long, etched in gold from the sun. As she came closer, he breathed her name. "Françoise, my angel." Indeed, she did appear angelic in her brown housedress and white pinafore—and barefoot.

"Stefano, I knew one day you would come." Her fingers trembled with the large key as she unlocked the gate. "You must come to the enclosed garden. Lucrezia strictly keeps the rules of quarantine. That is the reason we are all alive."

"Françoise, I have come to take you home in the carriage." He walked beside her in awe, relishing the pleasure of her nearness.

They entered the garden and sat on the same bench they had known before. Stefano noticed the neglect around him, how weeds had choked the flowers and grass had grown between the flagstones. "No deaths at all in the household— no servants?"

"They all deserted us, save one. Stefano, is your mother living?"

"Yes. She, Mira, and Sergio. They have been living shut up like this household. But they are well and the house cleansed."

"Thanks be to God. I pray for her continually." She looked down at her bare feet and tucked them under the bench. Blushing, she said, "I look like a peasant girl. We live quite informally now, somewhat like peasants, really. We all share the work equally, but it is good to stay busy. I hadn't finished dressing when the bell rang. I couldn't wait."

"Françoise, I have never seen you more beautiful." He ran his fingers through her long tresses. Her hair felt soft and clean, slightly damp with a faint hint of vinegar. "Those white, slender feet are lovely, too." He grinned. "And as your husband, I will be able to gaze at them all I want."

"And when will that be?" She smiled at him and lowered her eyelashes.

"The papers were drawn up along with the betrothal ones. I thought we might have a very simple ceremony at one of the chapels at the Duomo. As soon as possible. What do you think?"

"Simple, yes. Out of respect for the dead. But I would like to exchange our vows in the little chapel at the villa. Do you suppose the same priest is still alive?"

"I don't know, but I will inquire. I agree. Let's be married in the chapel where you and your dear mother worshiped—and Etienne. I grieve for them and your loss. I am so sorry."

He held her in his arms while they both wept softly.

twenty-two

After a time, Françoise went in, bathed again, and changed into clothing for travel. It didn't take long to pack her meager belongings and place a small box, which held a string of pearls, on top. She gave Cosimo's jeweled cross to Lucrezia. "I forgot again to give this to the duke's servant when he came for the letter. The jewels should be worth quite a large sum. And Stefano tells me Cosimo is sick unto death and we needn't worry more about him."

෨

At Stefano's request, Ferdinando came out to the garden and took a seat on a bench some distance from him. "I apologize for this impoliteness," Ferdinando said, "but we all survived by keeping apart."

"And I am forever grateful to you for saving Françoise along with your own. You have been a family to her," said Stefano with sincerity.

Stefano told Ferdinando that within a week the Marinelli villa would be completely deserted. "As soon as all danger has passed, Ferdinando, would you keep watch on the villa and, if possible, hire men to trim the gardens?"

Ferdinando agreed and expressed an interest in buying the villa if his business revived in the next few years. Stefano laid a pouch of money on the bench to cover caretaking expenses.

"I will send you a message when my bride and I are settled in Rome so you will know where to contact us. And I will be back to reimburse you for further expenses or make other arrangements as the circumstances require. I trust you fully, my good man."

෨

Ferdinando and Lucrezia helped Françoise transport her *cassone*, lute, and other belongings to the front gate, where Stefano helped her pack them in the carriage. Françoise ached to hug the children, but Lucrezia forbade it since she had been near Stefano. She bid the Maffei family good-bye with warm smiles and gratitude. By noon, the burdened carriage rolled back to the villa.

&

Sergio met them at the villa gate in an especially good mood. After greeting Françoise, he turned to Stefano. "You will find a pleasant surprise waiting for you inside." He bowed and took the reins of the horses.

"I like the word *pleasant* attached to surprise," said Françoise with a chuckle. "We don't hear those words together much anymore."

Stefano took Françoise's hand and hurried inside to see what awaited. When he opened the entrance door, they heard loud talking and much laughter coming from the small salon. When they appeared in the doorway, all sound hushed. Everyone arose and welcomed Françoise. Stefano's mother hugged her with tears of joy.

"My daughter, welcome," she said.

And there stood none other than Stefano's long-lost brother, Giulio! Stefano embraced him, gladdened to find him alive and healthy. "Now you must repeat your whole story for us."

"We were laughing at the antics of the students at the Sorbonne," said their mother. "But, Giulio, you must begin with your escape from the government militia."

"I was arrested along with Father—"

"Tell them your father's last words to you," interjected his mother.

"I will, Mother. I think there were about six soldiers guarding us when we stopped for the night and set up tents. Three of our friends in the network were captives, also. I lay next to Father that first night in the tent. Our two guards had fallen asleep. The others were in the next tent. I whispered to

Father, 'All is lost, isn't it?'

"Our hands were bound behind us, but he was able to turn over and face me. 'No, Son,' he said. 'Good work in the name of the Lord is never lost. Be at peace and sleep.'"

"I can hear Pietro's voice saying those words," said his mother, wiping her eyes. "That is just the sort of thing he would say for our comfort."

"The next day we met up with a larger group of the king's militia with wagons and more prisoners. An argument of some sort ensued. They put Father in a wagon and began questioning him. In the confusion, I slipped through the brush, my hands still bound. I had spent time hunting in the area and knew of a cave nearby with the entrance hidden. I crept in there and hid while they searched all around. By nightfall, they gave up. I cut my hands loose on a sharp stone and ran free."

⁂

Stefano learned of Giulio's return to the farm for supplies, his trip to Paris, and student life. More recently, Giulio had gone back to the farm and found Gaston and Claire managing well and collected the annual rent, which he then shared with Stefano and their mother. Stefano noted that his brother had matured a good deal through his hardships. On his way to Milan, Giulio spent some time visiting with their aunt Josephine in Bordeaux.

"She wants us to come live with her," he told his mother.

"But isn't she still angry that Pietro put us all in danger?" she asked. "I must feel free to speak kindly of him. Besides, Stefano has assured me a place with him and Françoise."

"Josephine still holds prejudice against the Huguenots, but she expressed only admiration for Father's courage," said Giulio. "She spoke fondly about memories of Father bringing her to France along with our family. I believe she truly misses you."

"Mother, you will always be welcome with us," said Stefano. "But we will have a small place in Rome at least for the first year. Josephine has plenty of empty rooms. Perhaps later, when we become more established, you can join us."

"Then I will accept Josephine's invitation," said his mother.

"I will miss you," said Françoise. "But please plan to be with us in Rome as soon as we have a larger place."

Thus it was decided. Giulio and Isabella would wait a few weeks for all plague to disappear, then go by coach and by sea, accompanied by Mira and Sergio, to Bordeaux to live with Aunt Josephine and her husband. Stefano learned that before his uncle Matteo became ill, he had laid his last will and testament on the table in the library. He read in it that a portion of his estate would go to his daughter, Lydia Capello, in Rome and to his wife, Caterina (if she were still living); the rest would be divided among his sister-in-law, Isabella Marinelli, and his nephews, Stefano and Giulio Marinelli. Stefano was named executor and would withdraw and distribute the funds.

Stefano's next days were crowded with business affairs, which included contacting a priest to perform the wedding ceremony in the villa chapel. The previous priest had died, he learned. Among all the activity, each person shared his story of what had happened in the time apart. Happiness seemed to reign; for though they told of the past, they looked toward the future.

৯৪

The afternoon before the wedding, Françoise strolled in the villa gardens, now overgrown with vines and weeds. The idle fountains were caked with algae and the statues streaked with bird droppings. Yet she felt pleasure in being there. *It's a miracle of God that joy can emerge amid all my sorrows*, she thought. She turned and saw the man who had brought such joy walking toward her up the path. He took her hand, and she smiled up at him.

"Isn't it amazing how quickly God's earth becomes disheveled without man's care?" observed Stefano.

"And our lives without God's care," said Françoise.

"I'm amazed you have kept your faith in God through all

you have endured." He put his arm about her as they walked.

"I haven't always. I felt God was very distant much of the time, even when I prayed. I believed my guilt separated me from Him, and though I prayed for forgiveness, I could not find peace." Françoise discovered that her words flowed effortlessly, unlike the many times before, when she had found it difficult to open her heart to him.

"Why should you feel guilty? I am the one who abandoned you. Even though I knew Etienne was sick, I left that morning for Florence," said Stefano.

"Let me tell you what Mira shared with me while you were off tending to business this morning. Her story will help you as it did me." She squeezed his hand and looked up at him.

"I told her of the guilt I felt for not telling Mamma sooner that we knew about cases of the plague. Mira was a mere girl when it struck Milan in 1530. She said she often heard the older relatives moaning over their guilt. They should have done this or they should not have done that. Someone might have lived if only they had been there."

"If only I had been here," said Stefano. "That is exactly how I feel. I should have realized the gravity of Etienne's illness. We knew about the plague."

"We knew, Stefano, but we didn't accept it," said Françoise. "Mira said her elderly aunt was one of the first to succumb. At the graveside, the priest told the grieving family—all guilt-ridden because they had not taken precautions—that in such extreme circumstances, a person cannot take in all the threatening horror at once. In our minds, we know tragedy will happen, but we refuse to accept it as real."

"That is exactly what I felt. I think I convinced myself we hadn't even seen the bodies being placed in the cart—or if we had, they'd died of other causes."

"When I finally realized others had thought as I," said Françoise, "I began to realize God was not punishing me for my neglect. I still do not understand why some were taken and others left. But I know God never abandoned me."

"I will think about this. So far I have not forgiven myself." He paused and moved to another subject. "Will you be happy in Rome?"

"I hear it is a beautiful city. But, Stefano, I will be happy anywhere as long as I am with you. Your aunt Caterina wanted us to find their daughter, Lydia Capello. She is married to a nobleman in Rome."

"We will find Lydia. And we will discover Rome together, you and I." They sat on the bench with the curved dolphin armrests, where they could look out over the city of Milan. Even in the coolness of approaching autumn, the sun felt warm across Françoise's shoulders. Stefano pulled up the dry weeds around the bench to keep them from snagging her skirt. "I love the smell of the soil. I am still a farmer at heart."

"I remember the first time I ever saw you," said Françoise, smiling. "You and Giulio were coming across the fields carrying hoes, and I thought you were from the king's militia. Then next I saw your gentle eyes across the breakfast table and knew I had nothing to fear from you."

"I found you attractive and mysterious then. I knew I loved you that last night at our farmhouse. When you and Etienne sang psalms, I knew I wanted to spend my life with you." Stefano circled his arm about her shoulders and kissed her with a fervor that matched her own. She surrendered herself to his embrace.

"Stefano, it was tragedy that silenced my heart for so long and kept me from fully trusting you—but now tragedies have opened my heart more fully. I could become bitter, but the love and trust I held for my parents and the care and love for my brothers and sisters still live. I don't understand it, but God has helped me feel that love for you—without reservation."

"I love you, Françoise."

"I love you, too, Stefano, with all of my heart."

A Letter To Our Readers

Dear Reader:

In order that we might better contribute to your reading enjoyment, we would appreciate your taking a few minutes to respond to the following questions. We welcome your comments and read each form and letter we receive. When completed, please return to the following:

Fiction Editor
Heartsong Presents
PO Box 719
Uhrichsville, Ohio 44683

1. Did you enjoy reading *Silent Heart* by Barbara Youree?
   ❏ Very much! I would like to see more books by this author!
   ❏ Moderately. I would have enjoyed it more if

   _____

   _____

   _____

2. Are you a member of **Heartsong Presents**? ❏ Yes ❏ No
   If no, where did you purchase this book? _____

   _____

3. How would you rate, on a scale from 1 (poor) to 5 (superior), the cover design? _____

4. On a scale from 1 (poor) to 10 (superior), please rate the following elements.

   _____ Heroine   _____ Plot
   _____ Hero   _____ Inspirational theme
   _____ Setting   _____ Secondary characters

5. These characters were special because?_____

_____

_____

6. How has this book inspired your life?_____

_____

_____

7. What settings would you like to see covered in future
   Heartsong Presents books? _____

_____

_____

8. What are some inspirational themes you would like to see
   treated in future books? _____

_____

_____

9. Would you be interested in reading other **Heartsong
   Presents** titles? ❑ Yes   ❑ No

10. Please check your age range:
    ❑ Under 18   ❑ 18-24
    ❑ 25-34   ❑ 35-45
    ❑ 46-55   ❑ Over 55

Name_____

Occupation _____

Address _____

City_____ State_____ Zip_____

COLORADO

4 stories in 1

Taming the frontier is a daunting task—one that can't be burdened by the luxuries of life, including romance. Four settlers take the challenge and are surprised when love springs up beside them along the way.

Four complete inspirational romance stories by author Rosey Dow.

Historical, paperback, 464 pages, 5 $^3/_{16}$" x 8"

♥ ♥ ♥ ♥ ♥ ♥ ♥ ♥ ♥ ❤ ♥ ♥ ♥ ♥ ♥ ♥ ♥ ♥ ♥

Please send me ____ copies of *Colorado*. I am enclosing $6.97 for each. (Please add $2.00 to cover postage and handling per order. OH add 7% tax.)

Send check or money order, no cash or C.O.D.s please.

Name _____

Address _____

City, State, Zip _____

To place a credit card order, call 1-800-847-8270.

Send to: Heartsong Presents Reader Service, PO Box 721, Uhrichsville, OH 44683

♥ ♥ ♥ ♥ ♥ ♥ ♥ ♥ ♥ ❤ ♥ ♥ ♥ ♥ ♥ ♥ ♥ ♥ ♥

$\mathcal{H}$EARTSONG ♥ PRESENTS

Love Stories Are Rated G!

That's for godly, gratifying, and of course, great! If you love a thrilling love story but don't appreciate the sordidness of some popular paperback romances, **Heartsong Presents** is for you. In fact, **Heartsong Presents** is the premiere inspirational romance book club featuring love stories where Christian faith is the primary ingredient in a marriage relationship.

Sign up today to receive your first set of four, never-before-published Christian romances. Send no money now; you will receive a bill with the first shipment. You may cancel at any time without obligation, and if you aren't completely satisfied with any selection, you may return the books for an immediate refund!

Imagine. . .four new romances every four weeks—two historical, two contemporary—with men and women like you who long to meet the one God has chosen as the love of their lives. . .all for the low price of $10.99 postpaid.

To join, simply complete the coupon below and mail to the address provided. **Heartsong Presents** romances are rated G for another reason: They'll arrive Godspeed!

YES! Sign me up for Heart♥ng!

NEW MEMBERSHIPS WILL BE SHIPPED IMMEDIATELY!
Send no money now. We'll bill you only $10.99 post-paid with your first shipment of four books. Or for faster action, call toll free 1-800-847-8270.

NAME_____

ADDRESS_____

CITY_____STATE_____ ZIP_____

MAIL TO: HEARTSONG PRESENTS, P.O. Box 721, Uhrichsville, Ohio 44683
or visit www.heartsongpresents.com